Mystery
of
Spider
Mountain

Mystery of Spider Mountain

A Hamilton Kids' Mystery

Jean Henry Mead

ISBN: 978-1-931415-30-9

First edition: February 2011

Second edition: August 2011

Cover design by Bill Mead

Produced by Medallion Books and printed in the U.S.A.

Dedication:

In loving memory of my grandsons,

Coleby Anderson and A. J. Johnson

Chapter One

"Jaime, look at this weird spider!" Danny yelled from where he had crouched beside the trail.

"Don't touch it," his thirteen-year-old sister warned.

Sam, who was eleven, rushed past Jaime to squat beside their brother. "Cool, dude," he said, pulling a small magnifying glass from his pocket. "That's a trapdoor spider."

Grinning, Danny used a twig to flip the Spider over. Jaime grabbed the twig and scolded him. "You know what Dad said about harming wildlife."

Ignoring her, Danny leaned closer, his blond hair hanging over his forehead. "Look at its big bubble head."

"The spider's building a trapdoor to her home," Sam explained.

Danny squinted at his older brother. "How do you know it's a girl spider?"

"Boy spiders have longer, skinnier legs and a redder belly."

"But how'd you know that?"

"Sam's a walking encyclopedia," Jaime said. "You should know that by now."

Smirking, Sam said, "They're called *Bothiocyrtum californicums*. They spin silk to hinge the trapdoors and hide inside their holes. When insects come along, they jump out and eat them."

"Yuck." Tired of watching the spider at work, nine-year-old Danny got to his feet and headed back down Spider Mountain. It was nearly time for dinner and their parents would soon be home.

Jaime heard Sam yelp in pain. Turning to look back up the trail, she saw a small owl perched on his head.

"Hoot owl," Danny yelled.

Sam reached up to brush the owl away. "Barred owl," he said, rubbing his injured head. In the fading light he looked like a younger version of their father, with dark hair and eyes and a slender build.

Jaime rushed to look at his scalp, and saw that one of his ears had been scratched. Why would an owl land on Sam's head? She watched the owl fly past Dead Man's Tree toward the mountain's summit. Did the people who lived there send the owl to scare them away? The dark house, surrounded by massive evergreen trees, was only one of the mysteries of Spider Mountain.

It wasn't really a mountain at all, but a huge, sloping hill inhabited by all sorts of crawling creatures. Even for a bookworm like Jaime, it was an exciting place to explore.

One of her least favorite creatures to find was a tarantula. The huge spiders grow as large as a grown man's fist, with long, hairy legs like bent pipe cleaners. Tarantulas sometimes ventured into the yards at the foot of the

2

mountain. There they climbed the sides of houses and perched on roofs where they watched the children play.

"Tarantulas come from Central America on banana boats," their father said one evening at dinner. "You shouldn't pick them up because they have a wicked bite."

Danny grinned. "I could trap one in a box."

Sam sneered at his younger brother. "What would you use for bait? A cheeseburger?"

Ignoring Sam, he asked his father what tarantulas eat.

His father set his fork aside. "Insects, as far as I know, son."

Sam pushed back his chair and rose from the table. "Anthropoids can eat animals as big as birds and lizards."

"Stop showing off, Mister Know-it-All." Danny looked back to his father, who was smiling.

"It's good to know as much as we can about our surroundings," he said. "Sam's a smart boy. He'll go far in this world if he continues to read and learn."

Danny made a wry face. "But why does he always try to make me feel so dumb?"

His father reached to draw Danny near. "You're smart about others things. But it wouldn't hurt to read a little more."

"I'm too busy." Danny said as he left the table.

Jaime noticed that he hadn't eaten most of his dinner. Her youngest brother must not be feeling well. She hoped a spider hadn't bitten him. Excusing herself, she followed Danny to his room. She found him sitting on his bed, head lowered and held in his hands.

"What's wrong?" she asked, massaging his back. "Are you sick?"

3

"No." He raised his head as a tear slid down his plump cheek.

"Don't let Sam get to you. You know how mean he can be."

"What can I do, Jaime?"

She thought for a moment. "Why don't you just laugh when Sam acts superior?"

"He'll hit me if I laugh at him."

Danny's shoulders slumped and he looked as though he were going to cry.

"I'll talk to Dad," she said, hugging him. "He'll know what to do."

She pulled Danny's pajamas from his dresser drawer. "Get some sleep," she said, tossing them on the bed. "Tomorrow we're going to climb the mountain to check on the house at the summit."

Danny smiled and wiped his tears with a sleeve. "Promise?" he whispered back.

"It's our secret. We won't tell Sam till morning."

Chapter Two

Jaime awoke with the first rays of sun and tiptoed to her brothers' room. She was anxious to get an early start. Both boys were sleeping so she returned to her own room. Rummaging through the cedar chest at the foot of her bed, she found an old pair of binoculars her father had given her. They would come in handy.

By the time she had dressed and gone to the kitchen for a bowl of cereal, she heard her brothers arguing. *Why can't they get along?* Setting her empty bowl aside, she returned to their room. Tapping lightly at the door, she waited. The howls coming from the room got louder as she pushed the door open.

"If Mom and Dad were here, you'd really be in trouble," she said, pulling them apart.

Too bad their parents had to leave so early for work each morning. She almost wished it were the weekend and they were home all day. Almost, because Jaime wasn't sure they would allow her planned trip up Spider Mountain.

The boys were squirming and trying to hit one another.

Letting them go, she said, "All right, get dressed. We're going to spy on the people in the dark house. Whoever gets ready first will carry my binoculars." She pulled them from the strap around her neck and held them high out of reach.

"Me," Danny yelled as he hurriedly pulled on a T-shirt and jeans. While he was fumbling with his shoe laces, Sam announced that he had won.

"Not fair," Danny whined. "You have pull-on shoes."

"Let Danny carry the binoculars." Jaime glared at Sam. "Why do you always have to win?"

"Because I'm the best." Sam puffed up his narrow chest, thumping it.

"We'll see who finishes breakfast first. Then I'll decide."

The boys rushed past her to the kitchen to grab their favorite cereal. Jaime sighed and shook her head. Her brothers were nearly more than she could manage. Opening the cupboard doors, she tried to decide which snacks to take on their climb.

"Potato chips," Danny said, with a mouthful of cereal.

"I'd rather have doughnuts." Sam left his stool to reach for a bag in the cupboard.

"We'll take apples and bananas," she said, "and cookies for dessert."

Both boys groaned.

"You're no fun," Sam placed his bowl in the sink.

"Grab some bottles of water and your backpacks," Jaime told them. "Let's get started."

Blue lupines waved in the cool breeze when they crossed the road and climbed the mountain's sloping apron. Before long, the heat of the August day would force them

6

to find shelter beneath a tree. Jaime hoped they could complete their climb before that happened.

When they had climbed as high as Dead Man's Tree, Danny set his backpack aside to grab a thick, knotted rope which hung from an overhead branch. Swinging out over the sloping terrain, he dropped into a huge pile of dried grass, yelling like Tarzan.

"Quit horsing around," Sam said frowning. "We have more important things to do."

"Like what?"

Jaime sat them down beneath the tree. "I told you we're going to spy on the people who live in that house," she said, pointing to the summit.

"What if nobody's home?" Danny placed the binoculars to his eyes and squinted.

"At least we'll know if anyone lives there."

Sam laughed. "You think we'll find a space ship?"

"Who knows what we'll find," Jaime said, getting to her feet.

They soon crossed over the narrow road that wound its way up the mountain. Choked with rocks and weeds, the road had not been used for a very long time. So how did anyone get to the top? In a helicopter?

Danny complained that his legs were tired from climbing, so they sat on a rock ledge and looked out over the southern California coastline. A patch of blue in the distance was the Pacific Ocean and the tiny dots moving across the harbor were ships sailing out to sea. Perhaps the ships would return with boatloads of bananas and crews of tarantulas. The thought made Jaime shiver. Thank heavens they hadn't met a tarantula on their climb up Spider Mountain.

7

"I'm hungry," Danny whined.

Jaime unzipped her backpack and handed him a cookie. Sam shook his head so she shouldered the pack and motioned her brothers to follow. The slope was now steeper and they were forced to dig the toes of their shoes into the crumbling earth. They used rocks and exposed roots for handholds and their clothing was already dirty.

Jaime twisted her neck to look back at her trailing brothers. Something slithered across her hand. Gasping, she jerked her hand and nearly lost her balance. She wondered what had possessed her to take this unexplored route. She then remembered. They could not be seen by anyone in the mysterious house.

"I'm stuck," Danny wailed.

"Stuck? How can you be stuck?" Jaime twisted her neck to look back down the slope. Her brother's sleeve was caught by a hanging branch.

"Help him, Sam," she called.

"Why should I? Climb down and help him yourself."

Jaime bit her lip. Why was Sam so mean? Reaching for a nearby limb, she carefully lowered herself to a ledge. The rock was long and narrow but she managed to keep from falling. Before she could reach to untangle Danny's sleeve, he yanked himself free, tearing the sleeve of his new shirt. What was she going to tell their mother?

"Keep going," Sam yelled. "I knew I should have taken the lead."

So now he was challenging her. "I'm going," she said. "Be quiet. We don't want them to know we're coming."

Sam, who was last in line, grabbed at Danny's shoe, which pulled from his foot and slid down the slope.

"Now look what you've done," she shouted.

"Keep quiet," he said. "The people in the house will hear you." He was smirking at her.

Jaime gritted her teeth. "Okay, the trip's over. We're going back home."

Her brothers yelled, "No!"

"I'm not taking two rowdy boys into a possibly dangerous situation. If you can't go quietly, we won't go at all." She shook her finger at them. "What kind of spies make so much noise that the enemy hears them coming?"

"Captured spies." Danny hung his head.

Jaime glared at them both. "I'll give you one more chance. If you misbehave again, we're going home."

Sam made an ugly face before he turned and scrambled to retrieve Danny's shoe. When it had been returned and tied, they continued up the slope.

Chapter Three

They heard dogs barking when they reached the summit. Tired and dirty, they rested behind a large evergreen tree. Jaime touched a finger to her lips, warning her brothers not to make another sound. The last thing they needed was to be attacked by a pack of vicious dogs.

Wiping hands on her jeans, she signaled them to do the same. She then removed her backpack and quietly unzipped it. Danny immediately reached for the remaining cookies and she jerked them from his reach. Offering him a piece of fruit, she watched as he peeled the banana and stuffed half of it into his mouth. It was a wonder he didn't choke. Then what would she do? Drag Danny's lifeless body back down the mountain?

The dogs were barking again. They must have been heard stepping on dried pine needles when they reached the summit. Peering around the tree, she hoped whoever lived there would not come out of the house.

In the shadow of the large evergreen trees, the house's weathered siding looked like it was made of gingerbread. If it were gingerbread, the dogs would have eaten the house by now. They were running back and forth inside the wrought iron fence, barking as though an army were invading. Four huge dogs with dark brown fur and heads the size of basketballs. Their jaws seemed large enough to swallow a child whole.

A door opened and a deep voice yelled to quiet the dogs. A large, scruffy man then left the house to look around. Ducking behind the evergreen, Jaime slid into a sitting position and lifted a finger to her lips. When Danny leaned to look for himself, she pulled him back and placed a hand across his mouth. Jaime's heart felt as though it were going to pound from her chest.

The man was talking to someone with an even deeper voice. "The dogs probably spotted a squirrel."

"Better look around just in case," the second man said.

"The old road's blocked. How could anybody get up here?"

"They could have climbed up or used an ATV."

The first man laughed. "We would have heard an engine. And why would anybody climb up here?"

"Wouldn't you if you knew what's in the house?"

"Yeah, you're right. Grab a gun and we'll have a look around."

Sam frantically signaled Jaime, mouthing, "Let's get out of here."

Nodding, Jaime led the way; glancing back to make sure the trees blocked them from the men's view. When they reached the edge, she slid down the slope until she reached a rock ledge. Swiveling, she looked back to find her brothers. Sam was behind her but Danny was nowhere in sight. Swallowing hard, she turned to climb back up the slope. She then heard a cry for help and someone calling her name.

Danny!

She saw her brother the moment she scrambled over the edge on hands and knees. Lying on the ground, Danny was staring up at a lanky man with stringy hair pointing a gun at him.

"Don't shoot. He's just a kid," she yelled, scrambling to her feet.

"What are you brats doing up here?" the man said.

"We were just exploring the mountain."

"What mountain?"

"Spider Mountain," Danny said, still flat on his back.

"T-that's what we call this big hill." Jaime said, trembling. "We didn't know anyone lived up here."

He lowered his gun and took a step toward her. "Didn't you hear the dogs barking?"

"Yes, sir," she said. "We thought they were lost and we were going to take them home." Jaime crossed fingers behind her back to nullify the lie.

"Well, they ain't lost and you'd better get yourselves back home."

"And don't come back." A smaller man appeared from a massive tree behind him.

"We won't," she said, meaning every word. She quickly offered Danny her hand and pulled him to his feet. Together, they raced back to the slope and slid down to the rocky ledge where Sam was waiting. Laughter echoed from the summit.

"What happened?" Sam asked.

"Later," she said. "Let's get out of here."

Taking the lead, Jaime slid most of the way on her back pockets. Their clothes were ruined and she would have a lot of explaining to do when laundry day came around. Their parents would be worried when told of the men with guns on the mountain. She felt nauseated when she thought about telling them what had happened, imagining the punishment awaiting her.

She dreaded them knowing how she'd let them down. They trusted her to take care of her brothers and keep them out of harm's way. Sighing, she dusted herself off and turned to do the same with them.

When they reached home, her hands shook so badly that it took a while to unlock the door. Still trembling, she herded the boys into their bedroom and told them to change clothes. If she didn't tell her parents what had happened, the boys certainly would. She heard the boys fighting again and rushed to their room.

Sam was twirling his dirty jeans in the air as though he were a cowboy throwing a rope. Danny ducked too late and cried out in pain when Sam's jeans struck him on the side of his head. Jaime grabbed the jeans and yelled at them both. Ordering them to sit on the floor with their backs to one another, she counted to twenty before telling Danny to take a bath. If she looked as bad as her brothers, she was going to spend considerable time in the shower.

Their grandmother was coming for a visit soon. Maybe she could talk her into staying forever. The boys loved their grandmother and would do whatever she said. Jaime had to find a way to convince her to move to the foot of Spider Mountain.

Chapter Four

Danny raced to the door as soon as their parents arrived. Before she could stop him, he told them what had happened.

"A bad man was going to shoot me," he said, out of breath.

Their mother looked to Jaime who was shaking her head.

"Please come into the living room." Jaime gulped back her fear. "I'll tell you exactly what happened."

"Good luck with that," Sam said from somewhere behind her.

When she finished the story, with interruptions from both her brothers, she burst into tears.

Her mother sat down beside her. "Do you know how foolish and dangerous it was to take your brothers up there?"

Jaime nodded and hung her head.

Sam crossed his arms across his chest. "She almost got us killed."

"That's enough," their father said. "Jaime knows what she did was wrong and you're not entirely blameless, Sam. You could have refused to go along."

"But you told us to mind Jaime and do what she said."

Their father sighed, his large brown eyes briefly closing. "Sometimes you have to use common sense. You knew that your mother and I wouldn't have allowed you to go up there, without asking."

Sam glared at Jaime and hung his head.

"It's my fault, Dad," she said. "I didn't realize it was going to be dangerous."

"Are you absolutely sure that what you told us is true?" He eyed each of them in turn. "Or is this a made up story?"

"Why would we lie about it?" Jaime said.

"Then we need to call the police. Those men could have killed you and buried you all up there."

"Who would believe a bunch of kids, anyway?" Sam's lower lip protruded.

Jaime burst into tears and ran from the room. She could hear the boys yelling at one another but their voices were soon silenced. Dad must be lecturing them. Falling across her bed, she muffled her sobs in her pillow.

A soft knock sounded at her door and she knew it was her mother. A hand soon stroked her back and a voice she could barely hear said, "We're going to have to ground you for the next two weeks."

Horrified, Jaime turned onto her back, hastily wiping tears. "Susan's birthday's next week," she said. "I can't miss my best friend's party."

"I'm afraid you'll have to, dear. If we don't punish you for what you did, it will set a bad example for your brothers."

"But, Mom—"

"The boys are grounded, too."

"Does that mean we're confined to the house until school starts?"

"I'm afraid so."

Jaime turned back onto her stomach and resumed her crying.

"It's not the end of the world. The time will go by before you know it."

"That means I can't shop for school clothes."

"Oh, I think we can make an exception for that. And I haven't told you the good news."

"What good news?" Jaime said, sitting up.

"Grandma is coming to live with us."

"She is?"

When her mother nodded, Jaime reached to hug her tightly. Everything was going to be all right with Grandma there.

"But we need to call the police and report what happened on the hill."

"The mountain?" Jaime said.

"Yes, your mountain."

"We were trespassing, weren't we?" The last thing she wanted to do was tell the police what had happened on the mountain. What if they arrested her for trespassing?

17

"Yes, you probably were. We'll talk to your father before we decide what to do."

Jaime sighed with relief. She would make Dad understand how dangerous it was for anyone to climb the mountain. The police would have to use a helicopter. Maybe not. She remembered one of the bad men saying that someone could use a four-wheeler.

She followed her mother into the living room where her father was talking to her brothers.

"Two weeks?" Sam was angry and turned to glare at Jaime.

"That's right, son. What you did was very serious and could have gotten you killed."

"But it wasn't my idea."

Their father lowered his head and sighed heavily. "If Jaime had jumped off a cliff, would you have done the same?"

Sam thought for a moment. "No, sir," he said. "That would have been stupid."

"What you did today wasn't very smart and I want the three of you to have plenty of time to think about it."

"But what will we do in the house all day?" Danny wailed.

"No TV or video games, but you can read and play board games."

"How boring."

"Get used to it, son. That's how you'll be spending the next two weeks."

"Grandma's coming," Jaime said, excited.

Both boys whooped for joy and their sister sighed with relief. She wasn't happy about their grounding, but Grandma loved to play games so it wouldn't be so bad.

She then remembered the men with guns in the house on Spider Mountain. What if they came looking for them?

Chapter Five

The police arrived half an hour later. Two of them. Taller than her father and heavier. She had been told not to be frightened but she had already envisioned herself in handcuffs in the back seat of the patrol car. A trespasser in custody.

"So you're the young lady who led your brothers up the hill," one of the officers said.

"Y-yes, sir," Jaime lowered her head and stared at her clasped hands.

"Why?" he asked, leaning his blond head in her direction.

"We wanted to see if anyone lived there."

"Didn't you know that you were trespassing on private land?"

"I thought the house was abandoned. We never saw anyone up there before."

The officer plucked a pad from his pocket and began taking notes. "Can you describe the man with the gun?"

Jaime looked briefly at her brothers, who appeared as frightened as she was.

"He was tall and thin with messy dark hair and wrinkled clothes."

"How tall?"

"About as tall as you are, sir."

"Did you notice the color of his eyes?"

"Dark."

"His skin color?"

Jaime bit her lip. Closing her eyes, she tried to remember what the man had looked like.

"I believe it's called ruddy, but maybe his face was red because he was mad."

The officer smiled and Jaime felt her muscles begin to relax. He then turned to Sam.

"Your name, young man?"

"Samuel J. Hamilton, the first."

"What's the J stand for?"

"Justice," he said, grinning.

"Sam," his father scolded.

"Sorry," he said, somewhat contrite. "Samuel Joseph Hamilton."

Jaime stared at him in disbelief. This was no time to show off.

"Did you see the man holding the gun?"

"No, I was down the hill, but my brother Danny saw him." He turned to his younger brother. "Tell him, Bro."

Danny's eyes brightened as he sat up straight in his chair. He told the officer that he had been grabbed by the arm as he was running for the cliff. The man had thrown him to the ground and threatened him with the gun. His description of the man was slightly different from Jaime's but he had been looking up at him from flat on his back.

"And the other man?" The officer looked back at Jaime, who described him as short, sandy-haired and dirty. She couldn't remember anything else about him because she had jerked Danny to his feet and run for the cliff.

Jaime told them what the men had said about something hidden in the house. When the officers left, she sighed with relief that she hadn't been arrested. Following her brothers onto the porch, she watched the patrol car turn the corner and disappear from sight.

"Why aren't they going up there?" Danny said, pointing to the mountaintop. "Don't they believe us?"

His father placed a hand on his shoulder. "They'll file a report and send someone else to investigate."

"What if those men come down here to find us?" Jaime said.

"We'll make sure the security alarm is set before we go to bed. And you kids will have to keep the doors and windows locked while we're at work. No one goes outside for any reason, understand?" He stared at each of his children with concern in his eyes.

"No problem." Sam's smirk had vanished.

"When's Grandma coming?" Jaime asked.

Her mother frowned. "Not soon enough. Her plane arrives on Saturday. That's three days that you children will have to be on your very best behavior." Turning to her husband, she said, "I wish I could take time off work, but it's our busiest season."

Jaime hugged her mother. "We'll be fine, Mom. I'll make sure that no one leaves the house."

"Or gets inside. I'll keep my cell phone handy all day in case you need to call."

Jaime's dad checked his watch. "It's getting on past dinner time. Why don't we go to town for cheeseburgers and fries?"

Danny whooped at the news. "We haven't had cheeseburgers since my birthday."

Cheeseburgers and grounding, Jaime thought. It would be a difficult three days until their grandmother arrived.

Chapter Six

The boys were fighting again. Maybe she should just let them wear themselves out. No, that wouldn't work. Danny would get the worst of it. Too bad there weren't more bedrooms so each boy could have his own room. Now that Grandma was coming, she would have to share a bedroom with Jaime. Dad had been talking about a four-bedroom house but that was in the future.

Jaime turned the knob and opened her brother's bedroom door. "Out," she said to Sam. "Go read the encyclopedias."

"I've already read them," he said. "They're too old anyway. I need to go online and read the Wikipedia."

"You know what Dad said. Only books, board games and cards."

"Come on, Jaime—"

She picked up a book. "You stay in here and read while Danny and I play board games."

Her brother glared at her as he accepted the book.

Danny followed her into the living room.

"What do you want to play?" she asked.

"The Ouija board."

"That silly thing."

"It works," he said. "You can ask the first question."

Grudgingly, she agreed.

Danny set the board on the dining room table and they placed their fingertips on the planchett, a small heart shaped piece of wood with a window in the center. "What should we ask the board, Jaime?"

"How about 'Who are the men on the mountain?'"

The planchette began to move and stopped at the letter K. It moved on to the letter R. Two Os followed. It then stopped at the letter K again and ended with an S.

"Krooks?"

"Maybe the spirits can't spell." Danny rubbed the freckles on his nose and grinned.

"It spells as well as you do. Are you sure you didn't pull the planchette to those letters?"

He made the sign of a cross on his chest. "Honest."

"Okay. Ouija board, what are the men hiding in the house on the mountain?"

The planchette hesitated for a moment before it began to move. It spelled out "boxes."

"Boxes of what?" Her heart was beating faster. Maybe the Ouija did work.

The planchette stopped at C, then circled the inside board several times before it halted at an A.

The doorbell rang before it reached another letter.

"Don't answer it," Danny whispered. "It might be the bad guys."

"I'll peek out the window. Grandma might have come early."

When she reached the front window, she lifted a corner of the drapes and peered outside. All she could see was a pant leg and a large black shoe. It was definitely a man.

Quickly closing the drapes, she let out the breath she had been holding and rushed back to the table. "There's a man at the door. I don't know who he is and we're going to hide in the bedroom."

Before they could move, the bedroom door opened and Sam yelled, "Who is it?"

They both tried to shush him as Jaime pushed him back inside and closed the door. The doorbell rang again and she quietly explained what had happened.

"I wanna see," He tried to get past Jaime but she blocked the door.

"What if he's one of those men from the house? Maybe they watched us slide down the mountain. That means they know where we live."

Sam gulped and released his grip on the knob. "If that's the man with the gun, we're done for."

"Better call Mom," Danny said.

"No, call the police."

They crept into the kitchen where Jaime reached for the wall phone. Carefully punching in 9-1-1, she whispered into the receiver, "Send the police before the man at the door kills us."

The operator calmly asked for her name, address and more details. When Jaime quietly told her what had taken

27

place on the mountain, the operator said she would send a patrol car as soon as possible. They waited, crouched on the kitchen floor until they heard a siren wailing in the distance. She tried to restrain her brothers but they scrambled to their feet and rushed to the front window.

"They're here," Sam yelled.

The doorbell rang a moment later.

Jaime carefully unbolted the door and opened it. Standing on the porch was the same officer who had questioned them the afternoon before. She stepped back to allow him to enter the foyer.

Danny immediately asked, "Where's the bad man?"

"I didn't see anyone," the officer said.

Sam crossed his arms and lifted his chin. That attempted look of importance again. "The guy must have left when he heard the siren."

"You kids here alone?"

"Our parents are at work and we've been ordered not to leave the house."

"I ought to take you all downtown with me."

"To jail?" Danny squeaked. "Hey, that would be fun."

"No it wouldn't." Jaime shook her head. "It's my fault, officer. When that man came to the door, I was afraid he was going to kidnap us."

"That's what concerns me."

"We'll be fine," she said. "We won't answer the door until our parents come home."

"Did you arrest those guys on the mountain?" Danny asked, dancing with excitement.

"No one was home when the officers arrived."

28

"How did they get up there?"

The officer held up his hands and sighed when everyone talked at once.

"There's a trail on the other side of the hill, and I don't want you young people going up there again. It's too dangerous."

"Did they find out what's hidden in the house?" Jaime asked.

"Not yet. It takes time to get a search warrant."

"Grandma's coming to take care of us," Danny said.

"When?"

"Two more days."

The officer checked his watch. "I'll see that a patrolman keeps an eye on the house in the meantime."

"So you think we're in danger, officer?"

"It's just a precaution. Don't open the door for anyone until your parents get home. Do you understand?" He looked at each of them in turn.

"Yes, sir," they said, and watched him walk away. When the patrol car left the curb, Jaime said, "Let's get back to the Ouija board. I think we're on to something."

Chapter Seven

The planchette went a little crazy after the policeman left. It spelled words that even Sam couldn't find in the dictionary.

Danny yawned and stretched. "Maybe we should give it a rest."

Jaime sighed. "I guess you're right. We could all use a nap. I didn't sleep very well last night."

"Me, neither," Sam said. "Danny kept getting up to peek out the bedroom window. I almost tied him to his bed."

"I was just trying to see if the bad guys had any lights on."

"And?"

"None that I could see."

"You must have scared them off with your ugly mug, little brother."

Danny swung before Jaime could stop him. It wasn't long before the boys were wrestling on the dining room floor. Thank heavens Grandma would be there on Saturday. Jaime doubted that even she could control these two rambunctious boys.

They slept most of the afternoon and awoke not long before their parents returned from work. The Ouija board was still set up on the dining room table and Jaime carefully packed it into its box. Tomorrow they would have another go at it. In the meantime, they'd keep a careful watch with Dad's old binoculars on the house atop the mountain. If they noticed anything, they would call Officer O'Donnell. Jaime pulled his card from her jeans to make sure she still had his number.

Mom had called several times that day to make sure they were all right, but Jaime didn't tell her about the doorbell incident until both parents arrived at home. She didn't want her mother to worry. Jaime thought she could handle anything that happened, with the possible exception of her constantly fighting brothers.

Two more days until Grandma arrived. Jaime returned to her room to arrange for her new roommate. Twin beds made her room seem small. One of them was to accommodate Jaime's sleep-over friends. She'd have to move her stuffed animal collection to her closet shelf. Better yet, she'd box them up to make room for Grandma's things. It would be a tight squeeze, but well worth it. Jaime smiled in anticipation.

When her parents arrived home that evening, the boys raced to the door to tell them what had happened. Her parents looked to Jaime as though to say, "Why didn't you call us?"

"It was nothing I couldn't handle," she said, before they could ask. "Besides, a policeman has been driving by all day to check on us."

Her mother said, "I'd better stay home until your grandmother arrives."

"No, Mom. We'll be fine."

32

"We can get a dog to protect us," Danny said. "A big one like a Saint Bernard."

Dad tousled Danny's hair. "Not a bad idea, son. A friend at work asked me yesterday if I would take his brother's Australian Shepherd. He's moving into an apartment that doesn't allow pets."

"Yes!" the boys shouted.

Their father phoned his friend while Mom and Jaime prepared dinner. The male members of the family then left to claim the dog. When they returned, a handsome shepherd bounded into the living room, but shied away when Jaime tried to pet her.

"Don't get your feelings hurt," her father said. "Sam and Danny have been making friends with her for nearly an hour. Give Miranda some time to get acquainted."

Jaime made a face. "That's a strange name for a dog."

"It's a nice name. She's two years old, so it's too late to change."

"Okay, Dad. Miranda it is. She can sleep in my room."

"No," Danny wailed. "She's going to sleep in ours."

The boys were standing on the threshold, holding Miranda's things.

"Miranda will be patrolling the entire house," their father said, leaving no room for argument.

The following morning, Jaime awoke early and wondered why the house was quiet. No brothers fighting, not even the sound of birds singing. How eerie the silence was, as though there were no one else on earth. Stretching, she yawned and pulled the bedspread under her chin. It was cool for an August morning and she closed her eyes to enjoy the silence. It certainly wouldn't last long.

33

She had lain there thinking about her grandmother's arrival when a loud noise startled her. It was probably a shoe thrown against the wall in her brother's room. Or was it something else? She rose from her bed to peer through the window. Nothing was out there that she could see. Grabbing her robe, she walked barefoot into the living room to part the drapes. Still nothing. It had to be the boys fighting.

They were both asleep when she quietly opened their door. Miranda was also asleep across the foot of Danny's bed. How strange that the noise had not awakened the dog or her brothers. They had probably stayed awake half the night quietly playing with the dog.

Where had the noise come from? It must have been a car's backfire although everyone had gone to work by now.

Jaime set out bowls and lifted cereal boxes from the cupboard. The boys could get their own milk from the refrigerator. She took her breakfast back to her bedroom where she looked at the walls. She decided to take down her boy band posters because Grandma might not like them. Sighing, she rolled them up and placed them in the closet. Maybe it wasn't such a great idea for Grandma to stay in her room. The dining room could be converted into a bedroom and they would all eat in the kitchen.

She heard the noise again and was so startled that she dropped her cereal bowl. What a mess! The boys must have heard the sound because she heard them yell. Leaving the cereal mess, she ran down the hall to their room where she nearly tripped over the dog. Danny was crouched on the floor, the bedspread over his head. She found Sam staring out the window.

"What was that?" he said.

"It sounded like a cannon going off."

34

"Sonic boom," Danny said, still on the floor.

Sam was skeptical. "Could have been, but I doubt it."

Jaime clamped both hands on her hips. "Why?"

"It would have shook the house like an earthquake."

"Let's go look outside." Danny headed for the front door.

"We can't," Jaime said. "Did you forget we're grounded?"

"Just for a minute," he pleaded.

"No!" Jaime was adamant. "We'll look out all the windows."

They looked first from the bedrooms and then from the living room. Jaime noticed smoke rising from the mountaintop and pointed to it.

Danny pressed his nose to the glass. "Somebody blew up the house?"

Jaime frowned. "Could be, but who?"

"Maybe the police." Sam said.

Danny turned back from the window. "You think the bad guys are in a gun fight with the police? Like on TV?"

"It's possible," Jaime said. "Run and get Dad's old binoculars so we can have a better look."

When Danny returned with the field glasses, Jaime scanned the area as best she could. Smoke still rose from the area of the house but she couldn't see anyone moving about or a vehicle of any kind. Maybe it was a grass fire. But that wouldn't explain the loud explosions. What could it be?

"Sirens," Sam said.

She could hear low-pitched engine noise. They must be fire trucks, but how could they get up a steep trail on the other side of the mountain?

"They'll have to use a helicopter to put out the fire." Sam pressed his nose against the glass to peer down the street. Their house faced the mountain and there was nothing to block their view.

"I wish Dad were here," Jaime said. "He'd know what to do."

"I don't think so," Sam replied. "That house is going to burn down before anybody can get there."

"What about the bad men's dogs?" Danny reached to pet Miranda.

Sam laughed. "They're probably crispy critters by now."

Danny glared at his brother. "You don't care about anything, do you?"

"Sure I do."

"What? Books and computers?"

They heard another explosion and ducked as the window rattled. When they rose to look again through the window, they watched a large plume of smoke rise from the mountain.

Red lights flashed as fire trucks stopped and firemen pointed at the smoke rising skyward.

"Some fireworks," Sam said, grinning.

Jaime sighed. "Looks like there's nothing they can do."

Danny scratched his nose. "Tomorrow we can climb up there and have a look."

"Yeah," Sam said. "We'll have to go before Grandma gets here. She'd never let us climb the mountain."

36

Chapter Eight

When the smoke cleared, Jaime raised the binoculars to have a closer look. "The house is still there," she said. "I wonder what caused the explosions."

"Let's go see."

Sam smirked at his brother. "Not till the police leave, dummy. You want to get arrested for trespassing?"

"Tomorrow then."

Miranda barked and they all turned to look at her.

"She's probably hungry." Jaime reached to pet her but Miranda shied away.

"She doesn't like you, Jaime." Sam laughed as he reached for the dog's collar and led her into the kitchen.

"Girl dogs like boys better," Danny said, trailing after them.

Jaime sighed. "Then you can feed her."

They were filling Miranda's bowl with food when Jaime decided to fill one of her own with cereal. Her earlier breakfast was still feeding the carpet on her bedroom floor.

After she cleaned it up, they would have another round at the Ouija board.

Jaime coaxed Miranda into her room with a rawhide bone and the dog quickly lapped up the mess. Then, when everyone had dressed and made their beds, they gathered at the dining room table.

"I'll get the Ouija board." Danny opened a cabinet door.

Sam said, "While you were cleaning up your room, I read about Ouijas in the encyclopedia."

Jaime stopped as she was taking a centerpiece from the table. "Really? What did it say?"

"The first mention was in 1200 B.C. in China but it was called a Fuji. And in 540 B.C. a Greek philosopher named Pythagoras used the Ouija to hold séances. They called it a spirit board."

"Spooky," Danny said as he set the board on the table.

"What else did you learn, Mr. Encyclopedia?" Jaime envied Sam's photographic memory. No wonder he got straight As on all his report cards.

"They were called talking boards in the United States in the mid-19th century, and they used them to spell out messages. Sometimes they swung a pendulum over a plate that had letters around the edges. And a tablet was fixed with a pencil that wrote out messages like automatic writing."

"But does the Ouija really work?"

"The ancient people must have thought so or they would have stopped using it."

"Well, let's hope this one can tell us what's happening on the mountain."

When they had placed their fingers lightly on the planchette, Jaime said, "Ouija, tell us what's hidden in the house on top of Spider Mountain?"

The planchette slowly circled the board and came to rest on the letter C.

"That's what it did the first time," Danny said.

Jaime shushed him and repeated the question.

The planchette circled again and landed on A. It then spelled out CASH and stopped.

"Cash?" Sam said. "Money?"

"Bank robbers." Danny's face widened into a grin.

Jaime remembered watching a news report about the increase in bank robberies. "Maybe they're the ones robbing all the banks in the city?"

She then asked whether the men were bank robbers. The planchette circled and stopped on the word YES at the bottom of the board.

"Wow, we solved the mystery," Danny rose from his chair and left the room.

"Where are you going?" Sam yelled.

"To see if everyone left."

"I'm not so sure we should go," Jaime said.

"Why not? If the cops arrested the bank robbers, there's no reason we can't go back."

"I promised Mom and Dad that we wouldn't leave the house."

"How will they know?"

"I'll know that I broke my promise."

"Don't be such a spoiled sport, Jaime. You know you wanna go as much as we do."

"What if there's another explosion and one of us gets hurt?"

"The police probably set off fireworks to scare the bank robbers out of the house. They'll take them when they leave."

Jaime sighed. "I guess you're right but what if Mom calls while we're gone."

"We'll leave a message on the answering machine saying we stayed up all night playing with Miranda. And that we're taking a nap."

"That ought to get us another month of grounding."

"Come on, Jaime. It'll be worth it."

"The mountain has already cost me a great birthday party at Susan's house next week."

"So what have you got to lose?"

"Mom and Dad's trust."

"We won't be gone long. They'll never know."

Jaime bit her lip. "Let's ask the Ouija board if we'll get caught."

"Good idea."

The planchette circled five times before it landed on *No*. Had Sam deliberately pulled it there?

"See, what did I tell you? Let's go as soon as they leave up there."

Jaime knew she should refuse. Officer O'Connell said it was dangerous and their parents would have a fit. Maybe they could just climb to the edge of the cliff and look through the binoculars. They could then carefully climb down so they wouldn't ruin their clothes.

"Ask it how much money the bank robbers stole?" Danny said when he returned.

"Oh, all right. Ouija, did the robbers steal a million dollars?"

The planchette immediately stopped at *No*.

"How much money is hidden on the mountain?"

Many dollars, the board spelled out.

Frustrated, Jaime said, "More than ten thousand?"

Yes.

"More than a hundred thousand?"

Yes.

"Wow," Sam said. "Think what you could buy with all that money."

"A bigger house with lots of bedrooms," she said, imagining a mansion.

"And a dog house for Miranda."

The dog barked as if she agreed.

"I'll go see if everyone left." Danny patted his leg so that Miranda would follow. Within seconds he called back, "Somebody's still up there."

Jaime sighed with relief. Although curious about what had happened on the mountain, she was nervous about investigating. "Too bad," she said. "I guess we won't be able to go."

Sam grabbed her arm. "You said we could."

"What about the dog? We can't leave Miranda here alone. She might tear up the house while we're gone."

41

"We'll take her with us."

Jaime laughed. "A rock climbing dog? I don't think so."

Miranda's sharp bark seemed to mean she agreed.

"She can stay in my room. I don't care if she tears it up."

It's so messy, no one would notice if she did.

Brushing his hand from her arm, she said, "Oh, all right. After I do the dishes." She returned to the kitchen to load the dishwasher.

What happened up there? Did the police capture the bank robbers? I wonder if the explosions blew up all the money. Some of it might be in the trees that we can pick like fruit.

The boys were still at the window when she came back from the kitchen.

"What's happening?"

Danny turned toward her. "Nuthin'. We might as well go."

She took the binoculars from him and scanned the area herself. Small puffs of smoke still rose and scattered in the wind, but no one was milling around. From the corner of her eye, Jaime noticed a patrol car coming down the street, and quickly closed the drapes.

"They're still checking on us," she said. "That must mean that they haven't captured the robbers."

Sam lifted a corner of the drape and peered out. "The cop is probably as curious as we are about the explosions."

"He must have heard about it on his radio."

"Maybe he wants to see for himself," Jaime said.

Sam could be right. What's going on up there? Could whoever set off the explosions have gone by now?

42

"Put on your oldest clothes," she said. "As soon as Mom calls we'll climb the mountain. But don't expect to stay. We'll just look around and come back."

Both boys whooped and ran for their room, with Miranda close behind.

What am I doing? I know we shouldn't go but I have to see what happened.

They waited for more than an hour until the telephone rang. Jaime punched in the speaker phone so they could all listen to what their mother had to say. She sounded worried. "Is everything all right there?"

"Just fine, Mom." *I can't tell her about the explosions or she'll rush right home.*

"How's Miranda doing? Has she let you pet her yet?"

"Not yet, but she's fine. She keeps following the boys around."

"Give it a little more time, dear. She was raised by a single man and isn't used to us females."

"Okay, Mom. See you when you get here."

"Promise me you won't open the door for anyone. Not even your friends."

"What if Grandma gets here early?"

"Her plane is scheduled to arrive at 2:15 Saturday afternoon."

"We can't wait to see her."

"Promise you won't open the door?"

Jaime crossed her fingers. "Promise."

When she replaced the receiver, Sam said, "Let's go."

"I promised Mom I wouldn't open the door."

43

"Which door?"

"The front one, of course."

"We'll leave by the kitchen door," he said. "That should fix the problem."

Sam led the dog into his room and closed the door. Jaime then grabbed her backpack and followed her brothers outside and across the deserted street. If any of the neighbors had been watching the explosions, they had already gone inside their homes.

The wind was blowing the lupines' small blue flowers in a swirling pattern that made Jaime dizzy. As she took the lead and climbed the lower slope, she thought of a dozen things that could happen, including grounded for a month. Was it worth it? No, she told herself, but her curiosity was more than she could manage.

"Hurry up, Jaime. You're too darned slow." Sam climbed alongside and tried to take the lead.

"Get back behind Danny," she said, "or we're going home."

Glaring at her, Sam did as he was told. Maybe he was right. She was poking along deep in thought. Picking up the pace, she headed for Dead Man's Tree. Danny would have to stop and swing on the rope before they went any further. His friend told him it was bad luck to climb the mountain without first gliding out and dropping into the pile of grass. It was too dangerous to swing back because he might hit the tree. She prayed he wouldn't hurt himself again.

Danny surprised her when they reached the tree. "Do you s'pose the horse thief that got hanged on this tree watches when somebody uses the rope? His spirit, I mean?"

Sam laughed. "Not where he went, I'll betcha."

44

"Lots of innocent people were hanged in the old days," Jaime said. "If the hanged man wasn't guilty, he might be looking down at us."

The three of them looked skyward.

"Get it over with," Sam said, "so we can make the climb."

Danny gripped the thick rope in both hands and swung out over the grassy pile. Jaime held her breath until she saw him land and turn to smile up at her.

"Come on, dummy, let's get going."

"Don't call him that. You're giving him a complex."

"So what?"

"I don't know why you're so mean-spirited, Sam, but I've had enough of it. One more nasty remark from you and we're going home."

"Threaten me one more time and I'll tell Dad that you made us come along."

"Okay, that does it. We're going back."

Jaime started down the trail and helped Danny to his feet.

Both boys wailed, but she continued on down the trail until she reached the house. When she looked back both boys were missing. Were they hiding in the tall grass or had they climbed Dead Man's Tree just to frighten her? She ran back across the street and climbed the mountain's apron. Scanning the entire area, she could see nothing but dried grass and blue lupines blowing in the August wind.

Chapter Nine

Jaime glanced up into the tree when she reached it, but could see nothing more than a small bird perched on an upper limb. What could have happened to her brothers? Heart beating wildly, she sat down near the exposed roots and took a deep breath. There was no one in sight but she called them repeatedly. When they didn't answer, she began to cry.

After a few moments she got to her feet and decided to climb further up the mountain. The climb was difficult because her legs were tired from her previous trip. Glancing toward the summit, she could no longer see smoke rising or any activity at all. She hoped the bad men had been arrested and taken off to jail.

Jaime checked her watch. It was eleven-fifteen and Mom would probably call again after her lunch break. What was she going to do? She was certain she would find her brothers when she reached the summit, but how had they managed to climb so quickly out of sight? Closing her eyes, she listened but could hear nothing but the wind.

Half an hour's climb later she reached the cliff. Hesitating, she slowly turned her head to listen again. Hearing nothing, she pulled herself over the edge to survey her surroundings. Still on hands and knees, she noticed a small burned area off to her left with a metal pail in its center. The smell of gasoline wafted past in the wind.

The house stood unburned but the dogs had disappeared. What had become of them? She remembered their vicious teeth and shivered. Glad they were gone, she worried they may have attacked her brothers. A cold chill raced the length of her body as she fought back tears. What could have happened to Danny and Sam? She couldn't call them because the men with guns might hear her.

Undecided what to do, she got to her feet and took up position behind a giant evergreen so that she could better see the house. She soon moved to a tree near the front door. Dare she get any closer? Biting her lip, she left the safety of the tree to look around. No one appeared to be peeking from the windows so she darted through the opened gate. When she reached the front door, she slowly turned the knob. The door creaked open, which frightened her even more.

With the drapes drawn, the room was nearly dark as she edged across the threshold. She should have picked up a fallen limb to protect herself but it was too late now. Inching into the room, she bumped into a chair and stooped to rub her knee. Listening, she could hear nothing more than her own frightened breathing.

A smell like rotting garbage nearly gagged her and she squeezed her nostrils together with her fingers.

"Danny," she whispered, her lips trembling. "Sam? Are you in here?"

The dark silence frightened her and she retreated back outside. Where were they? Glancing at her watch she saw that it was twelve o'clock and heard the faint sound of the noon whistle from across the highway beyond her home.

Her fear turned to anger when she thought of the punishment awaiting her. How could her brothers do this to her? New hope surfaced. Maybe they had returned home after finding no one there. If they weren't home, she would wait for her mother's call, then bring Miranda back to sniff out their trail.

A twig snapped behind her. Before she could turn to investigate, someone grabbed her arm and twisted it behind her back. When she screamed, a bad tasting hand covered her mouth.

"Keep quiet, little lady," a deep voice said. "Or you won't see your brothers again." When Jaime nodded the hand then slowly released its pressure. He released her arm and gripped her shoulder, pushing her toward the house. When she hesitated, he again jerked her arm behind her back.

Jamie winced in pain. "All right, I'm going."

"Smart girl."

"Where are the boys?" Tears ran down her cheeks.

"You'll see," he said, opening the door.

He pushed her into a small, empty room. The light from the window blinded her and she blinked to clear her vision. From the corner of the room she heard a groan and squinted to make out the forms of her brothers. Crouched in a sitting position against the wall, they were tied with rope and gagged with wide gray tape. Breaking free of her captor's arm, she rushed to kneel before them.

"Are you all right?" she whispered.

Their eyes like huge disks, both boys nodded yes and she hugged them.

The man laughed. "We knew you'd come back when you saw the fireworks."

Jaime glared at him. "You set off all those explosions to get us back?"

"Yeah, and it worked."

"But the fire department and police came too."

"They couldn't get up the trail."

"But they have helicopters."

"They probably thought it was brats like you that set off some cherry bombs and leftover fireworks."

Jaime tried to get to her feet, but he pushed her down. "Stay where you are." The man reached for the tape and piece of rope. Recognizing him from their earlier visit, she cringed and sank against the wall.

"Behave yourself and you won't get hurt." His long, greasy hair fell across his face as he bent to grasp her wrists and tie them. Jaime considered kicking him in the legs and running, but if she got away, he would take his anger out on her brothers.

"We'll behave ourselves," she said. "When will you let us go?"

The man laughed as he tied her ankles. "Now, why would we do that, little lady? We can't have you kids telling about our stash."

"Stash? What stash?" she said as he placed tape across her mouth.

When he left the room, Danny and Sam squirmed, trying to loosen their ropes.

She shook her head, trying to warn them to be still. When she heard the door slam, she lifted her legs and slammed her heels against the floor. That got their attention. Edging her way close to Danny, she scooted until her back was against him. She then stretched her fingers to feel the rope that bound his wrists. Nudging him, she hoped he would understand that she wanted him to maneuver his back to hers. When he did, she began pulling at the rope, trying to loosen it.

She then turned her head to nod at Sam, who seemed to understand what she wanted. He rocked back and forth until his back was even with Danny's feet and began to tug at the rope around his ankles. Danny groaned and pulled away. She knew the ropes were tight enough to hurt him and decided instead to work on Sam. She managed to get Sam's attention and lowered her head in an attempt to convey her message.

Sam scooted in her direction. When they were back-to-back, she worked to loosen the rope around his wrists. She then heard the door open and they quickly moved back against the wall.

"The girl's in there with her brothers, the first man said. "I tied 'em up tight and they'll stay that way."

"Better check on 'em before we leave," a deep voice said.

Jaime nudged Danny and slumped forward. Closing her eyes, she pretended to be asleep, hoping her brothers would do the same. A moment later she felt someone tug at her rope.

"Good and tight," he said. "Check the others."

"Yeah, they'll hold till we get back."

Jaime dared not open her eyes until the front door closed. She heard the click of a key in the lock and watched Sam push away from the wall and scoot in her direction. He must also wonder how much time they had before the men returned. They would have to work fast.

Chapter Ten

Jaime had to remove the tape from her mouth. She rubbed the edge of her face against her shoulder and looked at Sam. When he nodded, she fell sideways and rolled toward him. Sam maneuvered until his hands were near her face. When she scooted close enough, he gripped the edge of her tape and pulled. She yelped in pain as the tape tore across her mouth and hung from one side.

"Your turn," she said.

It took several attempts before she was able to peel the tape from his mouth. "Let's get these ropes off. We can use our teeth if we have to."

"What about Danny?"

"Wait until our hands are untied so we don't hurt him."

Danny nodded in agreement. He must have heard Jaime's cry of pain.

"Okay, who's first?" Sam struggled to pull himself into a sitting position.

Jaime rolled over until her back was against him. "Pull on my ropes till they're loose."

"Me first," Sam insisted.

"Do as I say."

"You're always pulling rank."

"There's no time to argue. Those men could come back any time."

Sam grumbled but set to work. "They won't budge," he said after a few minutes.

"Use your teeth if your fingers are tired."

"What if I accidentally bite you?"

"Sam," she wailed. "Hurry before it's too late."

Sam repeatedly tugged at the ropes. "We'll never get out of here."

"All right, I'll untie you. Make yourself as small as possible."

When he rolled onto his shoulder, she noticed tears on his face. She knew he was embarrassed and pretended not to notice.

"Roll back onto your right side," she said, "and let's get to work."

After a few moments her fingers ached but there was still little slack in the rope. Maneuvering so she could grasp the awful-tasting rope in her teeth, she pulled as hard as she could as Sam moved forward. Jaime then rolled back into position and tugged again with her fingers. The ropes slackened. Pulling it downward, she told Sam to wiggle his slender hips. Sam continued to twist and turn until at last the rope slid free.

"You next," he said.

When she was at last untied, they both set to work on Danny. When he was at last free, she said, "Let's go," and rubbed her aching wrists.

When Danny tried to stand, he stumbled and fell forward, hitting his head on the floor. Howling, he allowed Jaime to help him to his feet.

"Are you hurt?"

"Yes," he said, holding his head.

"We'll fix your head when we get home." Sam grabbed his brother's hand and towed him from the room. Carefully opening the door, he peered around the frame. "Nobody out here," he whispered.

Before Jaime could answer, he pulled Danny outside and took off running. Danny quickly fell behind and Jaime took his hand.

"My head hurts," he said.

"We have to get off the mountain."

Danny bit his lip and jogged along beside Jaime as she followed Sam to the cliff. While they briefly rested on the sandstone ledge, Jaime noticed a lump rising from Danny's forehead. How was she going to explain that to her parents? They had to tell the truth but Mom and Dad would never trust her again. When Grandma arrived, she would be shocked and disappointed in the three of them. It would probably ruin their reunion.

"Go!Go!Go!" Sam yelled as he slid further down the slope.

Jaime took Danny's hand and they followed their dare devil brother. Before long they were on the mountain's apron.

"Oh, oh, we're in trouble," Danny said, groaning.

55

Their mother stood beside their car, parked at the curb.

Jaime squeezed his hand. "We've got to take our punishment. They'll go easy on *you* because you're hurt."

"You'll be grounded forever," he said, holding his head with his free hand.

"But we got away, Danny, so we should be celebrating."

"Whoopee." With that he collapsed into a field of lupines. Her father was suddenly there scooping Danny up from the flowers.

"You've got some explaining to do, young lady."

Jaime hung her head. "I'm sorry, Dad."

"We were just about to call the police when we saw you coming down the hill."

"If I had a cell phone, I could have called."

"Not until you're fourteen. You know that."

"But Sally has one and so does—"

"Today you proved that you're not grownup enough to have your own phone."

She was in enough trouble without arguing. Following her father down the slope, they crossed the street and entered the house. Her mother held the door open, her lips tight. Jaime knew she was more than a little angry.

Their father carried Danny into the living room and placed him on the couch. His eyes were open and he was groaning.

"What happened to him, Jaime," her mother asked.

"He fell."

"We'd better get him to the emergency room."

"No," Danny said. "I've just got a headache."

"I don't like the looks of that bump on your head." Turning to Jaime, he asked, "Where did he fall?"

"Long story, Dad. You'd better hurry Danny to the hospital."

Her mother agreed and rushed to get her purse. As they were leaving, Jaime and Sam were told not to leave the house under any circumstances. "Do you understand?"

"Yes, sir," they said in unison.

"Clean up and we'll talk when we get back. And take care of the dog."

They watched through the window as the car left the curb. "It's all your fault," Sam said.

"My fault?"

"You were in charge and you shouldn't have let us go."

"Okay, I'll take the blame. Now get yourself in your room and clean up like Dad said."

Sam took off down the hall and opened his bedroom door.

"You're really in trouble now," he yelled.

"Why? What happened?"

"Miranda destroyed my room."

Jaime followed him to his room where Miranda greeted them by jumping on them. She gasped. Pillow feathers were strewn about as though a blizzard had blown through an open window. Bedclothes had been chewed and shredded and the boys' Sunday shoes were reduced to small pieces of leather.

"I wonder if Mom saw this." Sam shook his head as he scanned the room.

"Wait until she sees what Miranda did to the couch. We'd better clean up this mess before they get home."

Miranda licked Jaime's face when she knelt to retrieve a pillow. She was such a sweet dog but why did she cause so much damage? *How would you like to be locked up all day in the boys' smelly room?* Reaching to pet the dog's furry head, she decided they needed some trash bags. On her way to the kitchen, she remembered Susan's party. Her parents would ground her for so long that she would probably miss her senior prom. Her lips trembled and tears ran down her cheeks.

Chapter Eleven

Jaime had just picked up the last of the pillow feathers when the front door closed. Stuffing the trash bag under Sam's bed, they left the bedroom to greet their parents. Danny was holding his head and Jaime wondered if he was working to get sympathy to lessen his punishment.

Their father frowned. "Danny has a slight concussion. He needs to take it easy for a few days. No roughhousing, you understand?"

Sam and Jaime nodded.

"Thank goodness your grandmother will be here tomorrow," Mom said.

Dad led the way into the living room and motioned them to be seated. "Okay, Jaime, tell us what happened."

She sighed, wondering where to begin. Glancing at Sam, she noticed that he had lowered his head to stare at the floor.

"We decided to climb the mountain to see if that house had been burned." She expected one of the boys to contradict her but they weren't saying a word.

Dad walked to the window to look out. "Looks like it's still standing."

"Someone set some fires in metal pots to make a lot of smoke, so we decided to come back home."

"And?" her mother prompted.

"We started back and then I don't know what happened. When I turned around the boys were gone."

All eyes focused on Sam, who shrugged and said, "They grabbed us."

"Who did?"

Sam grimaced. "Two guys put something smelly over our noses."

"We were tied up with tape on our mouths when we woke up," Danny said.

Both parents turned to Jaime. She told them about her trip to the summit and the man who captured her. Her mother gasped and looked horrified. "You mean it actually happened?"

"Yes, ma'am," Sam said, and his siblings agreed.

Mom jumped to her feet and reached for the phone. "We need to call the police. Those men might come here looking for you."

Dad took the phone and walked into the dining room. They could hear the sound of his voice but not what he was saying.

"I'll make sure the doors and windows are locked," Sam said, leaving the room.

Jaime's mother turned to her, a hand to her chest. "Do you understand what you've done?"

60

Jaime lowered her head and began to cry. "Yes," she sobbed.

"Go to your room and stay there."

Miranda followed Jaime down the hall and slipped into her room. "Don't think you're going to trash this bedroom too," she said.

The shepherd sat and looked at her with such sad amber eyes that Jaime knelt to pet her. "I don't blame you. If I was locked up all afternoon in the boys' room, I'd probably trash it too."

Sitting on the floor, she hugged Miranda and cried the rest of her tears. What would her parents tell her grandmother tomorrow? Would they ever trust her again? And what if the bad men tried to break into the house?

She hugged the dog. "You'd bark and scare them away, wouldn't you, girl?"

Miranda shook her head as though she understood.

The house was quiet until the doorbell broke the silence. Jaime held her breath and looked at the dog, whose ears were pricked at attention. Her deep growl frightened Jaime. A moment later someone tapped at the door and her mother looked inside.

"The police are here and they want to talk to you."

Jaime gulped and got to her feet.

"Leave the dog here."

"Not a good idea, Mom. She made a mess of the boy's room." Jaime didn't tell her about the hole in the corner of the couch. She was afraid Miranda would be sent to the pound.

"All right, bring her along."

When they reached the living room, two tall officers stood near the entry door. Jaime noticed their holstered guns. She hoped they wouldn't take her downtown for questioning.

"So this is the leader of the mountain climbers," one of the officers said, smiling.

Jaime relaxed enough to return his smile. "Yes sir, I led my brothers up there."

"We'd like for you to come downtown to look at some pictures. You can talk to the police artist," the taller man said.

"But-but," Jaime stammered.

"Your father will come with you. You're not afraid to ride in a police car, are you?"

"No, sir. Will you turn on the siren and the red lights?"

Sam came into the room saying, "I wanna go too."

"You can both come but no siren and lights this trip."

Sam's face fell but he followed them out to the patrol car.

Her father hugged her mother saying, "I hate to leave you and Danny here alone."

"We'll be fine. Miranda will protect us."

The dark-haired officer assured them that another police car would be patrolling the area.

"We'll have you home before dark," he said.

Mom nodded, saying she would report any suspicious activities to the police."

Apparently satisfied, Dad motioned for Jaime and Sam to slide into the backseat ahead of him. Jaime breathed in the rich scent of leather and thought the patrol car must be new. A wire screen separated her family from the officers.

"Is this where the criminals ride when they're arrested?" she asked her dad.

"Probably. That's why the screen is there, to protect the officers from the people they arrest."

The officer in the passenger seat turned to look at her. "Your dad's right. I hope neither one of you ever has to ride in the back seat of a patrol car again."

"This is fun," Sam said.

Dad frowned. "You wouldn't think it's fun if you were under arrest, son. Keep that in mind."

Sam leaned forward to peer through the wire screen at the lights and gadgets on the dashboard panel. A woman's voice crackled over the speaker, startling Jaime.

"Suspects spotted at the corner of Grand and Darby Boulevard," she said. "Proceed with caution. Suspects armed and dangerous."

"Is that them?" Sam asked. "The robbers from our mountain?"

"Probably not," one of the officers said. "And why do you think they're robbers?"

"They told Jaime they had some stash."

The officer chuckled. "Stash could be any number of things."

"Like what?"

"We'll talk about it down at the station."

Sam slid back in the seat and sulked. A stern look from Dad prompted him cross his arms and stick out his lower lip.

Chapter Twelve

The police station was crowded when they arrived. Jaime took her father's hand and stayed as close to him as possible. People were standing in line before the glass booths and some of them looked like criminals she had seen on TV. One of the officers led the way to a small office while his partner parked the patrol car. Once inside the viewing room, they were told to sit in plastic chairs next to a large table. Large albums of photographs were arranged neatly in rows and Jaime and Sam were told to carefully study each picture.

It seemed hours before they peered at the last photograph and were disappointed they didn't recognized anyone. When the officer returned, Jaime said, "There are a lot of mean-looking people in these books but none of them look like the robbers on our mountain."

Sam nodded his agreement.

"Let's go down the hall to see the police artist," the officer said. "The two of you should be able to describe the men who kidnapped you."

"We were kidnapped," Sam whispered to his sister as they followed the officer down the hall.

"Of course we were. What else would you call it?"

"Held hostage?"

"Same thing."

They stopped talking when their father cleared his throat.

The police artist was seated at an easel when they entered the room. He smiled and motioned them to his side. "Let's start with the shape of the first man's face," he said. "Did it look like an egg, a coconut or a square of chocolate?"

"More like a horse's face with a long stringy mane," Sam said.

The artist smiled and began to draw. When he finished, he said, "like this?"

"Kinda, but with not so much hair on top."

He erased some of the hair and began to draw eyebrows. "Are they thick and meet in the middle?"

"Yeah, like that."

Jaime was silent, trying to remember what the men looked like. Her brothers had seen more of them and Sam had a photographic memory.

"Does this look right to you, young lady?"

She remembered a mole on the right side of the man's face halfway between his nose and mouth. She showed him where to place it after he had drawn the man's facial features, according to Sam's instructions.

"Good thing you came along, Sam," the officer said. "You're the best witness we've had in quite a while."

Sam smiled and folded his arms across his chest.

Jaime groaned. Why did her brother have to be so conceited?

"Good boy," their father said, tousling Sam's hair.

The artist removed the picture he had drawn from the easel and handed it to the officer, who promptly left the room.

"Okay, kids, let's work on the second suspect."

"He was short and ugly."

The artist looked at Sam, saying, "I'm afraid that I need a better description than that."

Jamie remembered the man who had threatened Danny with a gun during their first trip up the mountain.

"He had sandy hair and a ruddy complexion," she said. "And he didn't smell very good."

The artist laughed. "What else do you remember?"

"Short, stubby hands and chewed fingernails."

"Let's concentrate on his facial features."

"A round face."

The artist drew a circle on his pad.

"Thick eyebrows but they didn't meet in the middle."

"Were they arched or straight."

"Straight."

"He had a fat nose," Sam said. "With a wart on the side." He pointed at the drawing to show the artist where to place it.

"Little beady eyes like a bird."

"Near his nose or far apart?"

67

"Near," Jaime said, "almost cross-eyed."

The artist looked skeptical.

"She's right," Sam said, smiling at her. "I forgot about that."

"Samuel J. Hamilton forgot something," Jaime teased.

"Well, I'm only human."

"I'll remember that the next time—"

"Okay, what about his mouth?"

Jaime said, "Cruel mouth."

"Thin lips and small mouth," Sam added.

"That's him," they both shouted when the artist finished.

"I'm going to be a police artist when I grow up, so I can help catch some crooks."

Jaime laughed. "I thought you were going to be an astronomer and study the stars."

"I can do both."

"The officer will take you home," the artist said. "Thanks for coming in."

The ride back home ended all too soon and they waved goodbye to the officers.

"Well, that wasn't so bad, was it?" their father said as he unlocked the front door.

Sam grinned. "It was fun. Let's do it again some time."

"I don't think so," Jaime said. "We would have to be kidnapped and once was enough."

"She's right about that, son. You might not be so lucky next time."

"Aw, they wouldn't really hurt us. Would they?"

"It sounded as though they weren't ever going to let us go."

"Don't tell your mother that. She's worried enough as it is."

Miranda met them at the door and leaped against Dad's chest. "Down," he said, sternly.

Jaime reached for her collar and led her into the living room. "Good girl. Sit."

To everyone amazement, the dog immediately sat.

"There's hope for her, after all." Sam reached to stroke her head.

Their mother arrived from the kitchen. "I'm glad you're home. There's a little matter of a chewed couch that we need to discuss."

All three children groaned. Danny stepped out from behind his mother crying.

"What happened, dear?" their father said.

Danny rubbed his eyes. "Mom found the hole in the couch and she wants to send Miranda to the pound."

"No," his siblings said. "She's a good dog."

"Good dogs don't chew up the furniture."

Dad put his arm around her shoulder. "I thought you wanted a new couch."

"I do but what if Miranda chews it up too?"

"Please don't send Miranda away," Danny pleaded.

"We'll take turns staying with her every minute." Sam sat to hug the dog. "She was just lonesome because we were gone."

Jaime wondered whether her mother knew about the boys' torn up bedroom. That would settle the matter once and for all.

"Please don't send Miranda to the pound, Mom. We promise we won't ever leave the house again without your permission," Sam said. "We've learned our lesson."

"No more fighting," she said, looking at both boys. "Or Miranda will have to find a new home."

Sam and Danny looked at one another and hung their heads.

Jaime smiled to herself, wondering how long the truce would last.

Chapter Thirteen

Their father stayed home with the dog when the family left for the airport. He said they would have to fence the rest of the yard, before they could leave Miranda alone.

They waved goodbye until the car turned the corner and headed for the highway. The airport was north of town and it would take half an hour to get there. When they arrived, the parking lot was crowded and they circled the other cars several times before they found a parking space.

Jaime worried they might miss the plane but her mother said there was plenty of time.

"All of you on your best behavior," their mother warned. "We want Grandma to feel at home. And remember what I said about fighting." She glanced over her shoulder at each of her sons.

"Yes, ma'am," they said in unison before scrambling from the car.

"Walk like young gentlemen."

Both boys slowed down and waited. Jaime hoped they wouldn't break their bargain with Mom. She loved Miranda and couldn't bear to part with her. She wondered if her mother would actually send the shepherd away, if the boys misbehaved.

Her mother motioned the boys to walk behind her and Jaime, but it wasn't long before they were both jogging past. Jaime caught up with them and warned them to slow down.

"Remember Miranda," she said. She decide that was a good saying. She could use it whenever she needed to keep them in line.

When they reached the security station, a sign said, *No Passengers Beyond This Point.* A woman's voice then came over the loud speaker announcing flight 1737.

Danny yelled, "That's Grandma's plane."

"Yes, dear. But it will be a while before the passengers leave the plane and come here to the baggage area."

Danny sat and frowned, repeatedly swinging his feet as though practicing to kick a football. Their mother sighed and Jaime wondered if she wished her boys were girls.

A few minutes later the first passengers appeared. Jaime stood with the others, watching for a small white-haired lady. She was the last one up the ramp and they nearly didn't recognize her. Grandma's hair was no longer white; it was flaming red and curly.

Jaime's mom gasped before she hugged her own mother. "What have you done to your hair?" Short and slim, Grandma had passed her looks on to her daughter and Jaime. But she was no longer blonde or gray.

"I was tired of looking in the mirror at an old woman so I decided to change the color."

Danny grinned. "I like it, Grandma. It makes you look like Ronald McDonald."

"Really?" Grandma laughed. "I guess we'll have to visit him one of these days."

Jaime and her mother glanced at one another and smiled. This was going to be more fun than she had anticipated. She wondered what her father would say about his mother-in-law's new hair. Jaime's friends would think it was cool.

After Grandma had hugged them all, she looked at Danny's forehead, which had turned purple, yellow and blue.

"Tripped and hit my head," he said. "It doesn't even hurt."

Grandma didn't look convinced, but said, "Let's grab my bags and I'll race you to the car. "

The boys giggled and each took hold of one of her hands. Jaime sighed, happy to have a grandparent who made her laugh.

The luggage carousel was loaded with all sorts of baggage. Grandma told them to watch for yellow pompoms on the handles of her luggage. When they came by, the boys each grabbed a suitcase and placed it on the floor.

"Is that all, Grandma?"

"No, there's a big box of goodies that I brought for my favorite grandchildren."

"But we're your only grandchildren," Danny protested.

"Here it comes." Grandma bent to scoop up the box and hand it to Jaime.

"It's as light as cotton balls," Jaime said.

"Well, of course, dear. That's because it's empty."

They looked at each other and laughed. Grandma was making a joke.

Adjusting her glasses, she said. "Let's leave this noisy place."

Sam led the way with Danny close behind. The suitcases didn't seem to slow them down and Mom was too busy talking to Grandma to notice how far they had gone ahead.

Jaime hurried to catch up with them. "Slow down, guys. Remember Miranda?"

Sam stopped and made a face. "Don't think you can blackmail us into being good," he said. "Mom wouldn't send Miranda to the pound."

"When she finds out what the dog did to your bedroom—"

"Come along, dears," Grandma said as she caught up with them. "We don't want to be late for our round of chocolate milk shakes."

"Yes!" both boys cried. Setting the suitcases down, they did a happy dance.

After a noisy session at the fast food restaurant, the boys scrambled back into the car, smiling and happy.

"You're spoiling us," Danny said, "and I like it."

"That's what Grandmas are for, dear, but we can't do this every day."

"Every weekend?"

"If you behave yourselves, I'll talk your mom into driving us here on Saturdays. How's that?"

"How good do we have to be?"

"No fighting for starters."

Both boys groaned and looked at their mother, who smiled. "Yes, I told Grandma."

Danny and Sam scooted lower in the seat and pouted.

It wasn't long after they left the airport that Jaime noticed her mother glancing in the rearview mirror. "A car's been following," she said. "I wonder who it could be."

Jaime and the boys turned to stare through the rear window. Light reflecting from the windshield prevented them from recognizing anyone in the car. "I hope it's not those men," Jaime said.

Grandma also turned in her seat to look. "What men?"

"We'll tell you all about it when we get home, Mother."

Cold chills raced down Jaime's spine. What if it was them? What could they do?

She noticed her mother's white knuckles as she gripped the steering wheel. Still watching the road, she handed her purse over the seat to Jaime. "Take my cell phone from the front pocket and call your dad."

"Yes, ma'am." Jaime's trembling fingers retrieved the phone and punched in their home phone number. When she told her father what they suspected, he said to hand the phone back to her mother.

Jaime watched as her mother nodded her head, saying "Yes, dear." She then set the phone aside and engaged the turn signal. The car then made a left turn.

"Where are we going," Sam asked.

"You'll see."

At the next corner, the car turned right, then made another right turn. "Don't turn around to look," she said. "The car is still following."

When they reached the next intersection, she made another right turn and pulled onto the highway.

"What's this all about?" Grandma said.

"Some bank robbers are after us," Danny said.

"Bank robbers? But why?"

"We'll tell you later," Mom said as she handed her phone back to Jaime. "Call 9-1-1 and ask for Officer O'Connell. Tell him what's happening."

Jaime did as her mother asked but when she asked for Officer O'Connell, she was told he wasn't there.

Now what are we going to do?

Chapter Fourteen

They were still quite a distance from home when the other car pulled alongside.

"Step on the brakes," Sam yelled. "Hit the car on the corner of the back bumper. That'll spin 'em around."

"No, son. It's too dangerous."

"Then hit the brakes and get behind them."

Her voice quavered. "I'll try."

Grandma rolled down her window and yelled, "We called the police. You'll be arrested soon."

Jaime was frantically calling 9-1-1 when the other car slammed into their right front bumper. They were jolted sideways in their seatbelts as their car swerved dangerously close to the shallow median ditch.

"Slow down and turn around," Sam yelled again.

Mom slowed the car to a crawl before turning onto the median between the north and southbound lanes. She made a U-Turn and they bumped onto the northbound pavement. The men in the other car did the same.

Jaime gripped the front seat. "Are you all right, Grandma?"

"I'm fine, dear. Are you all okay?"

Danny was holding his head. He must have bumped it on the side window, but he didn't say a word.

"We're okay, Mom. Keep going."

"Step on the gas. Don't let 'em catch us again," Sam said.

Jaime asked the dispatcher to send the police. "We're on the interstate headed toward the airport." She then described the other car.

"They're catching up with us again," Sam warned. "When they pull alongside, stomp on the brakes and get behind them."

Their mother made a gurgling sound and did as he suggested.

"Tighten your seatbelts," Jaime said, "and put your heads down so they can't shoot us."

"What about Mom?" Danny whispered.

Jaime closed her eyes and held her breath. It wasn't long before she heard the faint sound of a siren.

"Red lights," Danny yelled.

"Where?"

"On the other side of the highway."

"A highway patrolman?"

Sam reached to touch his mother's shoulder. "Flash your lights so he'll know it's us."

Mom punched the emergency flashers and they appeared on the dashboard.

"Where's the other car?"

Sam craned his neck to look. "It just turned off on a side road."

"Thank heavens," she said, pulling off to the side of the highway.

Grandma reached to pat her shoulder. "Are you all right, dear?"

"You were great, Mom," Sam said, smiling. "Dad'll be proud of you."

The cell phone rang, startling Jaime. When she answered, she heard her father's worried voice.

"We're okay. Here's Mom." Handing back the phone, she watched with her brothers as the patrol car drove across the divider ditch and pulled in behind them.

Sam quickly opened his door and ran back to talk to the officer. Jaime saw him pointing toward the side road the other car had taken. When Sam returned to the car he said, "The patrolman is calling in a description of the car to his headquarters. It's a good thing he was already headed this way when he got the call."

"My, aren't you the smart boy," Grandma said, smiling.

Mom turned in the seat to look at them. "Dad wants to know if anyone's hurt."

"Jaime turned to look at her brother. "I think Danny bumped his head again."

"Danny?"

"I'm tough."

"The patrolman is coming," Sam said.

Mom rolled down the window and looked up at him.

"Would you mind following me back to the station to fill out a report, ma'am?"

"Not at all."

"Is anyone hurt?"

"My son hit his head."

"I can call an ambulance."

"No," Danny said. "I'm not hurt."

"What about the car, ma'am? Is it drivable?"

When she told him about the front bumper, he walked around to inspect the damage. After inspecting the undercarriage, he straightened to his full height, smiled and motioned them to follow. He was young and Jaime thought he looked like a movie star.

When they reached the highway patrol station, they saw that it was smaller than the police station in town. Only three clerks sat behind a glassed-in counter and no one was standing in line. Much better, Jaime thought as they followed the patrolman to the first window. After filling out the report, her mother sighed and told them it was time to go home.

"What about the bad guys?" Danny said.

"The patrolman's going to lead the way. We'll have 24-hour protection until they catch those awful men."

"If they try breaking into the house," Grandma said. "I'll whack 'em a good one with a frying pan." Her red curls bobbed as she laughed and held the car door for them.

"You're the best, Grandma," Sam said as he slid into the backseat.

"Well, I certainly try."

"Keep an eye out for that dirty black car," Mom said.

When they arrived home, the boys raced from the car to the front door. They couldn't wait to tell their father what had happened.

Grandma managed to make it to the door before it opened. She cautioned the boys to wait until everyone was seated in the living room before they started talking. "I feel like I turned on the TV in the middle of a movie," she said. "I'd like to hear what's happened from the beginning."

Both boys said, "Okay." They'd wait until Grandma gave their dad a hug and he returned from the car with her luggage.

Miranda stopped short when she noticed Grandma and began to bark.

"I guess your dog doesn't like red hair," she said, offering Miranda the back of her hand to sniff.

Danny hugged his grandmother to show the dog she was welcome. That seemed to satisfy Miranda, who then jumped to give Grandma a big wet kiss.

"Well, isn't that nice," she said, petting the dog.

"You'll have to sleep in Jaime's room until next week, Mother. We'll be turning the dining room into a bedroom for you." Jaime's mom wore a worried expression.

"Oh, good. We'll be roomies, Jaime and I. Won't that be fun?"

"Yes, Grandma." Jaime managed a smile. It would be fun, if only for a week. With her grandmother there, maybe she wouldn't be so afraid if she heard a strange noise during the night. What if the police didn't capture the bank robbers? And why were they still hanging around trying to capture her and her brothers? It didn't make sense.

Dad brought in the suitcases and carried them to Jaime's room. When he returned, he said, "Now let's hear exactly what happened."

"If you don't mind, Harold, I'd like to know what this is all about."

"Certainly, Agnes. Sit down and we'll fill you in. It's a story you'll find hard to believe."

Jaime cringed, worrying what her grandmother would think of her disobedience. Would she still want to share her room after she heard the story?

Chapter Fifteen

Grandma frowned when her son-in-law finished telling her about the children's misadventure.

"Hmmmm," she said, smiling at Jaime. "Not the smartest thing you've ever done, dear. But I'm sure you learned your lesson."

Lips trembling, Jaime nodded wordlessly as she gazed at the carpet.

Dad cleared his throat and asked what had happened on the way home from the airport.

"Mom first," he said when they all began talking at once.

When Mom finished, the boys told their version, which Jaime thought was a bit exaggerated. Grandma then told hers, including yelling out the window.

"You saw the men, Agnes?"

"Not too clearly, Harold. The window was as dirty as the car. But I saw a long-haired man with a thin face. He looked angry."

Jaime had been sitting in the middle of the back seat and couldn't see much of what happened. "I was trying to call 9-1-1 and dropped the phone when their car hit ours."

"If you hadn't called the police, no telling what might have happened," Grandma said.

Their father looked at each one of them in turn. "None of this makes sense. Why risk arrest by hanging around and trying to kidnap the kids?"

Sam scratched his nose. "Maybe we saw something we shouldn't have."

"Like what?"

"I dunno."

Danny got to his feet. "Let's ask the Ouija board."

"Good idea." Sam rose to follow his brother.

"Ouija board?" Dad said.

"A game a friend gave Danny for Christmas."

Grandma smiled. "Harmless fun. It lets the kids think they're solving the mystery."

"I'm not so sure it's harmless. What if it actually channels spirits? We don't want any poltergeists hanging around."

"Oh, Harold," Grandma said, laughing. "That's an old wife's tale."

Danny already had the board spread out on the dining room table. "My turn to ask questions."

Sam grumbled as he placed his fingers on the planchette.

"We'll take turns," Jaime said.

Danny hunkered low over the table. "Why are those bad guys trying to kidnap us?"

The planchette circled and stopped in the middle of the board.

Tired of waiting, Danny raised his voice. "Spell something."

The planchette slowly circled and stopped at the letter K. It then spelled K-I-D-N-A-P.

"We know that," Sam said impatiently. "Tell us why."

The planchette hesitated before it spelled T-E-S-T-I-F-Y.

"Testify," Jaime said. "They're afraid we'll testify against them in court."

Sam nodded. "That makes sense."

"Makes sense to me." Grandma was standing behind them with their parents.

Mom said, "Ask the board where they are."

When Jaime asked, the planchette circled several times before spelling C-A-R.

"Where is the car?"

"H-I-G-H-W-A-Y."

"Which highway?"

"Y-O-U-R-S."

"Oh, dear." Mom turned pale. "They're coming back."

"Better call the police." Danny hurried to get the phone.

Sam rose from his chair saying, "They won't believe a Ouija board."

"You're right, son. The police would think we've lost our minds."

"But the Ouija board is always right," Danny protested.

85

Grandma took a seat at the table. "Most people think it's a silly superstition."

"But you believe it, don't you?"

"Let's ask another question." Grandma added two fingers to the planchette, which had nearly been abandoned.

"Who are you, Ouija? Give us your name?"

The planchette immediately answered Grandma's question by spelling S-P-I-R-I-T.

"Spirit? That's not a name." Danny removed his hand.

"You must have another name. Tell us what it is."

The planchette quivered slightly before spelling out B-A-G-N-O-M-I.

"That's more like it. Now, tell us, Bagnomi, how we can stop the bad men from taking my grandchildren?"

The planchette rested for a full minute before moving again. It circled the board seven times before it slowly spelled L-E-A-V-E T-O-W-N.

"Leave town?" Dad said. "We can't do that,"

"There must be another way." Grandma tapped the center of the planchette saying, "Take your time and think before you answer, Bagnomi."

The planchette was still for several minutes. It then spelled O-U-T-S-I-D-E Y-O-U-R H-O-U-S-E.

Sam banged his fist on the table. "What's that suppose to mean?"

"The bad guys are outside our house?" Danny got up from his chair and ran to the nearest window.

Jaime followed. "Lock the doors and windows. Hurry!"

"Good idea," Dad said, "even if Bagnomi's wrong."

Grandma and Mom were still sitting at the table when Jaime returned, their fingers on the planchette, which was moving. "The car's gone," they said. "They must have just driven by."

"Ask Bagnomi where they're going?"

The planchette spelled H-O-U-S-E.

"Which house?"

"H-I-L-L."

"Spider Mountain?"

The planchett dived to the bottom of the board and stopped at the word YES.

"They're back on the mountain?" Sam left for the living room's front window.

Mom's voice rose an octave. "But aren't the police watching that place?"

"They probably think the robbers left town."

"But, Harold, why would they go back there?"

"If they're the bank robbers, they might have left some of the loot."

Yes, Jaime thought. They wouldn't be carrying all that money around with them.

"But why bother with the kids?" Mom said. "It doesn't make sense."

"It's a mystery, all right." Grandma's red curls trembled when she shook her head.

"The mystery of Spider Mountain's what we've got," Danny sang to the tune of *She'll be comin' round the mountain when she comes.*

"My goodness, child, you're a song writer." Grandma reached to pinch Danny's cheek.

87

"I'm an amateur detective, like the Hardy Boys."

"Of course you are, dear. And with Bagnomi's help we'll solve the mystery of Spider Mountain."

"You really think so, Grandma?"

"Yes, indeed. Now, what else can we ask Bagnomi before he goes off duty."

"Will the men be arrested?"

Bagnomi answered YES.

"When?"

"F-U-L-L M-O-O-N."

"Run and get the calendar," Grandma told Danny.

When he returned, she scanned the calendar to find the next full moon.

"Oh, my," she said. "The last full moon was three days ago. We'll have to wait until next month for another one."

Chapter Sixteen

"The police will catch those guys before next month. Won't they, Dad?"

"I hope so, Sam, but you never know."

Mom removed her hand from the planchette. "We'll have to be careful."

"I'll put my baseball bat by the front door." Danny ran to get it from his room.

"And I'll keep an iron skillet handy." Grandma left to look in the kitchen cupboards.

"Miranda will chase 'em off."

Dad plucked his cell phone from his pocket. "Maybe Bagnomi's right. I think I'll ask my boss for an early vacation."

"Where would we go, dear?"

He scowled and set his phone aside. "Good question. Where can we afford to go?"

Jaime remembered a television ad. "How about a cruise to Mexico? It only costs $149."

"Times six people." Sam said.

"Sam's right. We'll have to go by car. But where?"

"San Diego," Jaime said. "We could go to the zoo."

"Still too expensive. How about a camping trip?"

"Yes!" the children shouted.

Their mother found a map. "The Sierras would be a nice, cool place to camp."

Grandma looked worried. "Don't they have bears up there?"

Jaime's parents smiled at one another. "We'll stay in a campground."

"Miranda will scare the bears away." Sam hugged the dog until she yelped.

"Then it's settled. I'll call my boss and explain why we need to leave."

Now Mom looked worried. "I hope my boss will understand."

"If she doesn't, tell her you'll find another job when we get back."

"I'll call her now," she said, taking out her cell phone.

After dinner everyone began packing. One small duffle bag apiece was their limit.

Mom and Grandma were packing food and storing it in a cooler. The trunk of the car would be full.

"What about Miranda?" Sam asked. "Where will we put her?"

Dad thought for a moment. "Grownups in the front seat and kids and the dog in the back."

"What about the camping stuff?"

"We'll strap it to the top of the car like we usually do."

"But what if the bad guys are watching?"

Jaime said, "We can sneak all the stuff out tonight and leave before daylight."

"Tying the camping equipment to the car in the dark won't be much fun."

"The moon's still full enough to see what you're doing," Grandma said.

"Too bad the garage is full of stored stuff. I'll pull the car around to the backyard to load everything up."

Everyone smiled and went back to packing.

Danny's bag was so full that he couldn't pull the zipper.

"What have you got in there, son?"

"Some shoes and stuff."

"You only need the shoes on your feet, a change of clothes and some extra pairs of socks."

Mom decided to pack the bag for him. "What's this? You're not taking the Ouija board along."

"Bagnomi will be lonesome if we leave him here alone."

"You're taking that game too seriously, Danny."

Grandma took the board game, saying, "I'll put it in with my things, dear. If it rains, it will give the kids something to do."

Danny hugged her. "I love you, Grandma."

"Okay," Dad said. "We'll stay very quiet and leave by the kitchen door to pack the car. But first, I'll take Miranda out to sniff around. She'll let us know if anyone's in the yard."

He attached a leash to the dog's collar, turned out the kitchen light and quietly opened the door. They all stood listening near the open door. A few minutes later Dad and Miranda returned. "No one's out there," he said. "Follow me. Quiet as you can."

Lights were on in the house next door and they could hear a TV set. The fragrance of Mom's roses wafted on the summer air from near the neighbor's fence. Thank goodness the neighbors didn't have a barking dog. Danny tripped and fell and Jaime nearly stumbled over him. Fortunately, he landed on his duffle bag. Helping him up, she whispered for him to bring up the rear.

When the trunk was packed, they trooped back to the house. Dad and Sam stayed behind to strap the tent and sleeping bags to the car rack. Half an hour later they returned.

"Time for bed," Dad said. "We'll be getting up before daylight."

The boys complained they'd miss their favorite TV show but soon disappeared down the hall to their room.

It was going to be a great adventure, Jaime thought, as she and Grandma got ready for bed. A camping trip was a good way to spend her grounding time. She hoped it wouldn't be extended when they returned.

Grandma's alarm clock went off at 4:00 a.m. Jaime groaned and went back to sleep. She soon felt someone shaking her shoulder. "Wake up, dear. It's time to go to the mountains."

"Too early," Jaime mumbled and pulled the blanket over her head.

"We'll have to use a flashlight to get dressed."

"A flashlight?" That brought Jaime out of bed. She had used a flashlight to read after lights out but had never dressed by one.

"I'll take my clothes into the bathroom," Grandma said. "There's a night light in there."

Jaime hoped her brothers wouldn't turn on a light to get dressed. Mom must have awakened them by now. It was spooky getting dressed in near darkness and she hoped she wasn't putting her clothes on wrong side out.

Everyone met in the kitchen where they ate granola bars. The light from the electric range hood provided enough light. Grabbing bottles of water, they left the house single file to pile into the car. Miranda was stubborn and refused to jump inside until Sam tossed a dog bone onto the seat.

"Buckle your seatbelts," Dad said before he backed the car from the yard.

Driving slowly down the side street, they had no headlights until they reached the highway. There were no other cars on the road and they joked about their escape. Mom was worried the robbers would break into the house while they were gone.

"Not with a police car patrolling the neighborhood," Dad said.

"Shouldn't we call the police and tell them where we've going?"

"Good idea, Marian. Better give them a call."

"We're not sure where we'll be staying," she told the dispatcher. "We're going to the mountains."

"Tell them we'll call when we're settled."

The boys had already dozed off by the time their mother finished the call.

"Any word about the bank robbers, Mom?"

"Nothing yet."

"They don't seem very smart—"

"Smart enough to escape capture," Dad said as he turned onto another highway. Dim light spread across the mountain peaks in the distance. Real mountains, not like their own. Before long the sun was streaking the sky ahead and her parents pulled down sun visors to protect their eyes.

Seated between the two boys so they wouldn't be tempted to fight, Jaime decided it was time for a nap. But Miranda had other ideas. She had slept on the floorboard under Danny's feet and was now ready to play. Licking Jaime's arm, she yipped and jumped into her lap. A lap full of Miranda was more than Jaime could handle.

"Stop the car, Dad. Miranda needs to get out."

Miranda showed her appreciation by giving Jaime a wet, sloppy kiss.

Chapter Seventeen

The first two campgrounds were filled but an unoccupied space was available at the end of a rutted trail. As soon as the car came to a stop, they jumped out and chased one another around the open field.

"They're tired of being cramped up," Grandma said as she eased herself off the seat. "I'm afraid I am too."

"Good thing we have extra sleeping bags," Jaime said.

"I hope the tent's big enough for all of us." Grandma looked closely at the tent, which appeared rather small in the car rack.

"Plenty big," Dad said as he unstrapped it. "It can easily sleep six."

"Sometimes we bring a friend," Jaime said.

"That's nice, dear. Let's set up camp."

After they had unloaded the car and staked down the tent, Dad glanced at his watch. "It's lunch time."

Mom remembered to call the police to tell them where they were camped. She tried various locations in the campground but her cell phone had no signal.

"Looks like we're on our own, dear."

"We'll be fine," he said.

"Sandwiches and chips for lunch." Grandma took them from the cooler. "Tonight we'll fry some hamburgers on the grill."

"What grill, Grandma?" Jaime looked about the campground.

"Oh, dear, I don't see one either."

"No problem," Dad said. "We'll build a campfire."

"Just like the pioneers. Living off the land. I hope I'm not too old for this."

Jaime smiled. "You're the youngest grandma I know."

Dad whistled and the boys came running back. "After lunch, we'll go fishing in the stream we passed down the road." The boys whooped with excitement.

"I didn't see any fishing poles," Grandma said.

Dad grinned. "We'll cut some limbs from the trees. The hooks and lines are in the glove compartment."

"I'm glad you're so resourceful, Harold. The children need to learn how to survive in the wilderness."

"I'm glad you agree."

"Even grownups can get lost in the mountains."

"They both have a compass in their pockets," he said, reaching into his own. "Here are three small ones for you ladies, although I doubt you'll wander far from camp."

Dad asked Jaime to go along but she decided to stay in camp to take pictures. After lunch, Dad and the boys hiked down the road toward the stream. Mom and Grandma settled in the tent to read and take a nap, so Jaime decided to explore the campground.

96

"Promise you won't go far," Mom said.

"I'm just going to take some pictures. I won't be gone long."

Jaime spotted a jackrabbit with huge feet hopping toward a grove of pine trees. She hurried after him. When she reached the trees a large, colorful bird flew into the upper branches farther into the grove so she made her way there. She then heard a rustling of limbs and noticed a spotted fawn trotting among the trees. She aimed her camera at the small deer but it disappeared before she could click the shutter. She followed it further into the grove.

A flock of birds took flight when she approached. She managed to click off one frame before they too disappeared. But where were the fawn and jackrabbit? They couldn't have gone far. The trees thinned a bit and she saw movement ahead on the edge of clearing. The animal was larger than the jackrabbit but too small for a deer. What could it be?

When she got closer she noticed a long ringed tail. The animal turned and looked at Jaime with dark, masked eyes. Quickly raising the camera, she snapped three pictures before the raccoon limped slowly into the underbrush. Jaime remembered reading about raccoons, who were nocturnal animals. Why wasn't this one sleeping during the day? It walked as though it were injured. She got down on her hands and knees to try to rescue it. She then heard a hissing sound.

Snake? She scrambled to her feet and backed away. Searching the ground she didn't see a reptile of any kind, so she looked around to get her bearings. All she saw were evergreen trees. Which way had she come? The ground was hard from lack of rain so there were no footprints to follow. Taking out her compass she turned until the needle was pointing north, but was camp in that direction? Deciding that south was a better choice, she started off into the woods.

There was too much foliage to walk a straight line, but she kept the needle as close to south as possible. Glancing at her watch she noted the time: 2:15 p.m. What time had she left camp? Probably one o'clock. The camp had to be close by. Tired, she sat down in the shade of a tall tree and drifted off to sleep.

When she woke, the sun was slanting low over the evergreens and she looked again at her watch. It was nearly five o'clock. Mom and Grandma must be worried. She called their names but heard no reply. Checking her compass, she headed north again; then stopped, noticing that the trees were no longer pine. She must be going in the wrong direction. She then turned south to retrace her steps.

A flock of birds flew overhead but she ignored them. There was no time to take pictures. She had to return to camp before dark. Picking up her pace, she dodged trees and forgot to recheck her compass. A grove of evergreens was ahead and she hoped it was the same one she had originally walked into.

Branches scraped her bare arms and jeans as she hurried into the grove. When she remembered the compass, she reached into each pocket and found it missing. It must have fallen out of her pocket when she stopped to take a nap. It was too late to look for it. She had to keep going. The sun was now hiding behind thick branches of trees. It would be dark soon. She stopped and yelled her family's names. Dad and the boys must be back from fishing by now. Maybe they were out looking for her.

"Dad," she yelled. "Sam! Danny!...Mom!...Grandma! Where are you?"

A tear hesitated on her cheek. She brushed it away and rubbed her eyes. She couldn't allow herself to cry. She had to find her way back to camp. Which way should she go?

She heard branches breaking off to her right. "Dad!" she screamed.

The noise stopped for a moment, then began again. Maybe it was an animal. She stopped breathing long enough to listen. The wind had picked up and was blowing from the direction the sun was setting. If it were an animal, she reasoned, she was downwind from it. Whatever it was couldn't catch her scent until it passed by. She needed to move away from the sun, which she glimpsed in small patches through the trees.

A huge evergreen loomed ahead and she took refuge behind it. She then heard a deep groan as two black cubs passed by followed by a large black bear. Holding her breath, she backed around to the far side of the tree and waited until the bears had disappeared from sight. Heart pounding in her ears, she sat on the hard ground to hold her head. She didn't dare call out again because she might attract another bear. Maybe even a mountain lion. She shivered at the thought.

Light was dimming when she started out again. If she couldn't find camp she would have to bed down for the night among the trees. If she survived, she would start out again at daybreak. A steep slope loomed ahead. If she climbed to the top, she might be able to see smoke from a campfire. But could she get there before dark? Jaime adjusted the strap on her camera and picked up a good-sized limb.

Chapter Eighteen

The slope was steeper than she had imagined. It was slow-going because the ground was covered with undergrowth. Tired from climbing, she found a bare spot beneath a tree and sat to rest. The sun's glow was fading from the horizon and she knew that darkness would soon arrive.

Forcing herself to her feet, she set out again, praying she could reach the top before she could no longer see well enough to climb. The wind had increased and her bare arms were cold. She knew she would have to find something to cover herself to stay warm. Twilight soon descended into darkness and she had not yet reached the highest point. Scanning the area, she could see no smoke trails or fires. How could she have wandered so far from camp?

When she tripped over a large root and fell, she knew she could go no farther. Groping in the dark for leaves and fallen branches, she settled under a thick-trunked tree and covered herself as best she could. Exhausted, she cried herself to sleep.

Jaime awoke at dawn, tired and itching from her blanket of leaves. When she got to her feet, she felt stiff and sore from her climb. Brushing herself off, she looked about for her camera before starting up the slope. Her stomach growled with hunger. When she finally reached the highest point, she scanned the area in every direction. It was probably too early for anyone to be starting a cooking fire, so she would stand there and wait until she could locate a column of smoke. Temporarily blinded when the sun showed itself from a mountain peak, she was forced to face the West.

Nothing seemed to be moving. The wind had calmed to a gentle breeze so even the branches were still, as though waiting for something to happen. There had to be someone in sight. If only she had a red flag to wave or a mirror to reflect the sun. She looked about but found nothing to attract attention.

Maybe she could start a fire. If Sam were here, he'd know what to do. Or Dad. She choked back a growing lump in her throat. As she stood waiting, she remembered watching a wilderness survival program. Starting a small fire was first on the list. She hoped she could remember the rest.

Jaime set about gathering small dead limbs and breaking them in short sections. She then formed a pyramid and filled the interior with leaves. She searched for some time before finding a sharply pointed rock as well as one with a smooth surface. Taking them back to her pyramid, she rubbed one stone against the other over the bed of leaves. But, although she created sparks, the leaves refused to ignite. She then pounded one rock against the other inches above the leaves. Still no fire. She would have to try something else.

She again scanned every direction, shielding her eyes from the sun as she squinted toward the East. Why wasn't someone cooking breakfast? At the thought of food, she realized how hungry she was and how very thirsty. If she had something to catch her tears, she could drink them to relieve her thirst. She laughed at the thought.

Trees were stunted on the rise but she noticed bushes growing on the slope to the south. Carefully climbing down and watching for poison ivy, she noticed dark green berries growing on a grove of spined bushes. Were they also poisonous or could she eat them? No small white flowers or serrated leaves were visible so they weren't the deadly water hemlock she learned about at Girl Scout camp.

They must be gooseberries. She picked one and had her hand scratched for her trouble. Rubbing it against her blouse, she took a bite and waited. Glancing at her watch, she decided that if it were poison, she would start getting sick within five minutes. When the time passed, she ate another berry and carefully picked a handful. Trudging back up the slope, she sat to eat the rest. No longer hungry, she realized that the berry juice had helped to relieve her thirst. Maybe she should camp there until someone found her.

Her family must be worried. She wondered how many people were out searching for her. If they found her, she would be grounded for the rest of her life, if she were still alive. Thank goodness it was mid-August and not the middle of winter. She shivered at the thought. It was much cooler in the mountains than at home. She wouldn't freeze to death, unless no one found her soon. She decided to renew her efforts at starting a fire.

Rubbing and pounding rocks made her scratched hands ache. Maybe they were the wrong kind of stones. Rocks were scarce here on the summit so maybe she should do some nearby exploring. She would first have another look around. Carefully scanning the entire area, she thought she saw a wisp of smoke, but decided it was only a small cloud. Had she walked so far that no campgrounds were in site?

103

She sat listening for sounds floating on the breeze. The only sounds were birds chirping and leaves rustling in the increasing wind.

What to do? If she wandered too far away, she might not make it back to the summit before dark. A wild animal might see her before she saw it. "I'd better stay put," she said aloud. The sound of her own voice frightened her. Would she ever speak to anyone else again? Her lips trembled and she allowed herself to cry.

Her watch said noon so another trip to the gooseberry bush was in order. Maybe she should look a bit farther to find something tastier than the same tart berries. Removing the strap from her shoulder, she set the camera aside. She then trudged back down the slope.

All the bushes looked alike so she would have to settle for gooseberries. Her mouth puckered at the thought. She consoled herself with the fact that they were better than eating leaves. Jaime climbed back up the slope with another handful of berries and fresh scratches from the nasty bushes. If only she were home on Spider Mountain, she would even make friends with a tarantula … or not.

It was only noon but it seemed as though she had been there a week. She was beginning to miss her brothers. How could that be? This was a real vacation from their yelling and fighting. Still she missed them and wondered if they missed her too.

Mom and Grandma must be worried as well as mad because Jaime had wandered off. She shaded her eyes and searched for any sign of movement. She knew that Dad was out there searching for her. She hoped he wouldn't get as lost as she was.

The sun warmed her body and made her sleepy. Crawling under the nearest tree that provided shade, she rested against its trunk and promptly went to sleep. When she awoke, the sun was sliding toward the trees. What time was it? Her watch said 5:16. It was nearly dinnertime. At the thought of more gooseberries, Jaime decided she wasn't hungry.

Scanning the area once again, she saw nothing moving in every direction but the West. The sun was bright going down and she would have to wait until twilight. Picking up the camera she wondered whether her pictures were good enough to print. She would ask for a digital camera for Christmas, if she got home alive.

"Wait a minute," she said aloud. "If the flash still works I can set it off in every direction as soon as it's dark. Maybe someone will see it." She felt silly talking to herself but considered it a brilliant idea. Even Sam could not have thought of something better.

While she waited for darkness, she gathered more leaves and made a bed for herself. I should have gone down to the evergreens and twisted off some branches, she thought. But it's too late now. When it was nearly dark, she turned on the camera and stepped to the edge of the summit, facing West. Clicking off one flash picture, she moved to where she thought it was South. After flashing each direction, she turned off the camera and sat down to wait.

Nothing happened. The moon should be up soon but there was even less light than the night before. There was nothing to do but sleep. Lying down on her bed of leaves, she scooped up handfuls to cover her bare arms. Shivering, her mouth felt as dry as a bag of potato chips. She should have eaten more berries.

A branch snapped somewhere behind her. She then heard what sounded like a growl. Too frightened to move, she thought about her camera. Where had she left it? If it were a bear or mountain lion, she could throw the camera at it and run. Or better yet, she could set off the flash and scare it away. Groping on the ground around her, she felt the strap and dragged the camera to her. Fumbling to turn it on, she got to her feet and waited. More limbs snapped and another growl sounded close by. Her hands were shaking so badly that she nearly dropped the camera. But she managed to aim it in the general direction and set off the flash.

The animal made a frightened sound and seemed to be retreating. Just to make sure, she clicked another picture, setting off the flash. Her heart pounded so hard that she couldn't breathe. Whatever it was, it must be blinded by the flash. But would it return? She tented her fingers and prayed.

"Dear God, please protect me from the wild animals and help the rescuers find me. I miss my family and I promise I'll never be mean to my brothers again. And I'll never climb Spider Mountain." That was a promise that wouldn't be easy to keep."

Chapter 19

Jaime held her breath until she was dizzy. Closing her eyes to listen, she heard a faint snapping sound in the distance. The animal must be running away. She hoped that it would warn other animals to keep their distance. But maybe it would make them curious enough to investigate on their own. She shut her camera off to conserve the batteries.

Even slight sounds made her tremble. When the moon's crescent sliced overhead, Jaime dozed off and dreamed of wolves and bears. She found herself in a tall tree with a huge bear climbing up toward her. When she screamed she awoke with cold chills. Clutching the camera, she lay watching the moon move across the sky, wishing for daylight. She had already decided to open the camera as soon as the sun came up. Removing the film, she would place the opened camera over the leaves so the lens could start a fire.

I wonder if Sam would think of that, she thought, smiling to herself. You're not the only smart kid in the family.

Jaime must have dozed off because it was dawn when she opened her eyes. The moon had disappeared and the sun would soon be up. Rising from her bed of leaves, she carefully removed the film from her camera and placed the roll in her pocket. Then, scooping leaves into a deep pile beneath her branch pyramid, she placed the opened camera face up in the middle of the mound.

While she waited for the sun to move to the right position, she would breakfast again on gooseberries. She first looked around for animal tracks but could find none in the dry earth. Rescuers would find it impossible to find her because she had left no tracks. Sighing in frustration, she made her way down the slope to the gooseberry bushes.

On the outer edge of the grove she noticed a small deer foraging on dried grass. Deer were too smart to eat the berries because the bushes would scratch their noses. She wondered whether Mom would bake a gooseberry pie. Jaime made a face. She was already tired of eating them. She would gladly trade her camera for a chocolate chip cookie. On second thought, she might need the flash again that night. What would she do when the batteries lost their charge? She didn't want to think about it.

When she returned to the summit and had eaten her fill of berries, she knelt on her knees to check her camera's progress. Nothing yet. The sun probably needed to be overhead. If the leaves did catch fire, she'd have to grab the camera before it burned. While she waited, she thought of her family and how much she loved them. Grandma could stay in her room as long as she wanted. And the boys could put on boxing gloves and duke it out in the living room. She wouldn't care as long as she was home.

She wondered if the police had captured the bank robbers. Or were they still hanging around waiting for the family to return? If they were still at large, they were much smarter than Jaime had given them credit. With all that money they had stolen, why didn't they buy a new car?

Maybe they did and that's why the police hadn't arrested them. Jaime thought for a while about capturing the criminals. There must be a way.

She heard a snap and saw a tiny flame. Grabbing the camera, she blew on the leaves that appeared to be burning. To her disappointment, the flame went out. Rearranging the leaves, she set the camera back in the pile and watched intently. She wouldn't blow on it again, but would allow it burn at its own rate. Before long she saw a tiny puff of smoke and picked the camera up to hold it above the leaves.

"Yes," she shouted when the leaves began to burn. She would have to continue supplying the fire with fuel to keep it burning. Setting the camera down a safe distance from the fire, she raced about picking up anything that would burn. She hoped she wouldn't have to burn her bed.

Jaime climbed down the slope to gather fuel for the fire. It was late afternoon and the fire still burned brightly. She hoped the wind wouldn't pick up and start a forest fire while she was gathering limbs. Arms loaded with everything she could carry, she thought about picking leaves from the trees because they would create more smoke.

"Why didn't I think of that sooner?"

When she trudged back up the slope, she began breaking limbs into small pieces. Satisfied the fire was contained, she began gathering green leaves. Some of the trees didn't want to let go and she had a tug of war with them. When she had an armful, she took them back to the fire and dropped one at a time. The smoke did increase and she wondered if someone would see it. She was beginning to feel that she was the only person left on earth.

The sun was setting when she heard a distant noise that sounded like an engine. A car couldn't travel among all the trees so it must be an airplane. She scanned the sky but could see nothing but an occasional bird wheeling its way among the air currents. Jaime sat down to fan the dying embers. She was too tired to climb back down the slope.

She then noticed a speck on the horizon, growing larger as it drew nearer. What could it be? She soon realized that it was a helicopter and began jumping and waving her arms. Afraid the crew might not see her, she hurriedly kicked the remains of her leaf bed into the embers, which immediately flared into a full fledged fire.

"Please see the fire. Please, please," she begged, resuming her jumping and arm waving.

The helicopter grew larger and she could see two men behind the bubble cockpit. One of them waved to her as the helicopter hovered overhead. A rescue basket was then lowered to the slope. Someone was telling her over a loud speaker to climb into the basket. Grabbing her camera, she slung the strap over her shoulder and reached for the basket, which was by now too high.

The wind from the rotor blades caused the fire to flare up again. Waving her arms, she pointed to the flames. "I'll try to put it out," she yelled although she knew they couldn't hear her. Racing back to the fire, she kicked the embers and stomped on them with her tennis shoes. Her pant leg caught fire and she dropped to the ground to extinguish the flames.

A helicopter crewman was lowered to the ground to make sure the fire was out. He then helped her into the basket. Jaime felt like hugging him but clung instead to the cables. She closed her eyes and screamed as the basket lifted skyward into the waiting chopper.

Strong hands pulled her inside where a crewman asked, "Are you Jaime Hamilton?"

"Yes, sir, I am."

"Your family's very worried about you. They're waiting at the campground."

"You're a famous young lady," the other crewman said.

"What do you mean?"

"Your picture has been in all the newspapers and on the television news. Everyone's been looking for you."

"Oh, no," she said, remembering the bank robbers.

Chapter Twenty

The helicopter ride didn't last long. Jaime peered from the opening to see a crowd of people on the ground looking up. Some waved as the chopper began its descent.

"Looks like quite a welcoming committee," someone said behind her.

Jaime groaned and ducked her head. How was she going to live this down? She hesitated before unbuckling her seatbelt when the aircraft touched down. Within moments the crowd she had earlier seen walked toward her, hunched over and whipped by the rotor wind. A flashbulb blinded her and someone asked how she felt.

Rubbing her eyes, she said, "I'm fine. Where's my family?"

"On their way. It won't take long."

A warm hand reached to take hers and help her to the ground. "You've landed at ranger headquarters," a uniformed man about her father's age said. "We've had searchers out looking for you ever since you disappeared."

Someone held a microphone near her face. "Are you all right? How did you survive?"

"Long story," Jaime said, edging closer to the ranger station. "Do you mind if I go inside?"

Everyone seemed to be talking at once and Jaime wanted to hide.

"This way," a woman said, taking her arm. When Jaime looked up, she noticed the uniform as well as a comforting smile.

"You must be tired and hungry."

"I've had my fill of berries but I could use some water."

"Coming right up." The ranger closed the glassed door behind them. Holding her hand palm up, she warned the others not to follow.

"You don't have to talk to them, Jaime."

"How'd you know my name?"

"Everyone who watches television knows it by now."

Jaime's lips trembled as tears began to fall. Collapsing into the nearest chair, she held her head at knee level.

"Are you hurt?"

"No," she said, sobbing.

The ranger knelt to stroke Jaime's back. "Do you want to tell me about it?"

"It was awful." She straightened and looked into the ranger's eyes. "But it was great too because I outsmarted the bears and an animal that was going to attack me." She lifted her camera, saying, "I set off the flash and scared him away."

"You were brave, Jaime. Did your parents teach you survival skills?"

"My dad taught us some things and I learned more in Girl Scout camp."

"That's great." The ranger knelt to hug her. "Are you sure you're all right?"

"Yes, ma'am." Jaime smiled through her tears. "I can't wait to tell my brothers how I started a fire with my camera lens."

Someone rapped at the glass insert in the door and lifted a TV camera. The ranger shook her head and pointed to her watch. "We'll wait till your parents arrive. Let them decide about an interview after they talk to you."

Jaime sighed with relief.

The ranger hurried to the back of the station. She returned a moment later with a bottle of water and a candy bar.

"A Hershey bar," Jaime exclaimed. "You don't know how much I've dreamed of one ever since I got lost."

"Can I get you anything else?"

Jaime smiled and shook her head, her mouth full of chocolate. She was feeling much better.

Before she finished eating, a car door slammed and her family appeared at the door. Jumping from the chair, she rushed forward to hug her mother first. When everyone else had been hugged, she told them what had happened since her disappearance.

"I'm sorry that I worried you," she said, gazing at the floor.

Her mother clapped a hand to her chest and sighed. "Don't ever wander off again."

"Not a chance, Mom. I've had my adventure of a lifetime."

"Tell us again about the bears," Danny said, grinning. "Were they this big?" He stood on his toes and stretched his arms as high as they would reach.

"The mother bear must have been taller than Dad, and the cubs were nearly as big as you."

"What about the animal you scared away?"

"Won't know till we get my film developed." Jaime pulled the roll from her pocket. "It's all here in living color."

"Maybe not," Sam said, looking a little jealous of all the attention Jaime was getting.

The man with a TV camera again tapped the glass.

"Are you willing to talk to the reporters?" the woman ranger asked.

Jaime looked to her parents who shrugged as if to say, "It's up to you."

"Do it," Danny said. "We can watch you on TV."

Jaime hesitated. "I don't know."

"Don't be a chicken," Sam said. "I'll go with you."

"Well, why don't *you* serve as the family spokesman so all the kids at school will think you're special. You can even sign autographs."

"Why not?" Sam smirked and wiggled his brows.

"Very funny, Samuel *Justice* Hamilton."

"We'll all go," her father said. "Let's get it over with or they'll be hounding us forever." He led the way outside and they lined up in a row. Dad held his hand for silence, then nodded to the nearest reporter.

"How did you survive the cold nights?" a blond woman asked.

116

"Leaves and dead branches," Jaime said, rubbing her arms. She was cold just thinking about it. "And my Girl Scout training."

When her father coughed, she said, "And the greatest dad in the whole world taught us survival skills."

Dad was suddenly surrounded by people asking him questions. Relieved to be out of the spotlight, Jaime walked back into the ranger station and asked for another candy bar.

"I don't want to make you sick," the ranger said. "How about a ham sandwich?"

Disappointed, Jaime reluctantly agreed. She took a seat near a window and watched the media circus taking place, glad that she no longer had a microphone under her nose. Sam was strutting around for the cameras and answering questions. Let him be the star.

Danny stood with his mouth open as reporters interviewed each family member. Even Grandma. Jaime was glad she couldn't hear them tell how worried they had been. That would come later when they returned home. The phone probably wouldn't stop ringing for a month. They might even have to change their number. What would her friends and teachers say when school started? And would the bank robbers still be hanging around?

It was all just too much and she was so tired. Her head soon slumped forward and she faded into sleep.

Chapter Twenty-One

An hour later, the TV crews loaded their equipment into a van and drove back down the mountain. The ranger advised her parents to take Jaime to a doctor as soon as they reached home.

"I'm fine," she protested, but the adults insisted. She needed to see Doctor Bryan.

"But what about the bank robbers?"

"We'll call the police," her mother said. "Maybe they've been arrested."

Grandma placed her hand on Jaime's shoulder. "If they're still around, dear, we'll keep our weapons handy. I'm pretty darn good with a frying pan."

Everyone laughed as they trooped out to the car.

"Short vacation," Sam grumbled, "and it's all because of you."

Jaime sighed. "I know, but at least the kids at school will think you're special."

Sam grinned sheepishly and dropped the subject.

119

"Tell me again about the bears," Danny said

Jaime repeated her ordeal on the mountain and the grownups praised her ability to survive.

"Using the camera lens to start a fire was brilliant," her father said, and even Sam agreed.

Mom turned to beam at her. "We're very proud of you, honey."

Jaime wondered aloud how the helicopter crew had found her.

"We don't know all the details," Mom said, "but someone saw the smoke from your fire and reported it to the ranger station."

"Not the camera flashes?"

"Another smart idea," Dad said, "but we don't know if anyone saw them."

"But weren't you all out looking for me?"

"Your father and the boys joined a search team, but Grandma and I stayed at camp in case you found your way back."

Jaime bit her lip. "I'm sorry I worried you."

Grandma said, "You didn't plan to get lost, dear. And your mother and I knew they would find you."

"How'd you know?"

Grandma laughed. "We used the Ouija board."

"You did?"

"Yes, indeed. We needed something to distract us while you were gone."

"The Ouija said that Grandma will be getting married again," Mom said, giggling.

"To who, Grandma?"

"I haven't met him yet, dear. I just know his name."

"Joseph P. Wainscott," the boys said in unison.

Jaime laughed. "Are you serious?"

"It must be true. The Ouija never lies."

Their father rolled his eyes.

Jaime leaned forward to whisper, "Did you ask about the bank robbers?"

Grandma nodded.

"And?"

"Ouija said we would capture them, ourselves."

"How?"

"We didn't get a chance to ask because a ranger came and said you'd been found."

Jaime leaned back against the seat and considered what she'd heard. How could they capture the bank robbers?

"I'll unpack the Ouija as soon as we get home," Grandma said. "Then I'll ask the board again."

"I'll help you," Danny said.

Sam had been surprisingly silent until now. "We'll outsmart 'em, all right. Anybody who hangs around a crime scene must be pretty dumb."

"Our house isn't exactly a crime scene, son."

"No, Dad, but it could be. We can set up all kinds of traps like putting the iron on top of a door—"

"One of us could get seriously hurt, like Grandma, who might forget it's there."

Grandma shook her bright red curls in agreement.

"I'm afraid we'll have to depend on the police to guard the house *and* us," Dad said.

Mom reached over the seat to pet the dog. "Miranda will guard us."

Jaime wondered if her mother would still be petting the shepherd if she knew about the mess in the boys' room. Hopefully, she already knew.

"Try your cell phone," Dad said. "We should probably call the doctor before we get home."

Mom tried but they were still in a no service area.

"Really, I'm fine. I don't need to go to the doctor."

"You heard what the ranger said, dear."

Jaime sank back into her seat and said little during the rest of the trip. When they rounded the corner next to their house, a large white satellite truck was parked in the driveway. Cars lined the curb in front of their house and Dad drove past without slowing down.

"More TV reporters," Sam said. "Why aren't we stopping?"

"We'll stay in a motel."

"Why?"

"The last thing any of us needs is to answer more questions. We all need some rest."

Sam groaned as he stuck out his lower lip.

My brother the publicity hound, Jaime thought as she leaned her head against the seat. Maybe Sam would become an actor. Then he could live in front of the cameras. She stole a glance at his profile. She had to admit that he was handsome, in a weird sort of way.

"What if the reporters are still there tomorrow?" Danny said.

"I'm afraid we'll have to talk to them, son. We can't stay in a motel forever."

"Well, at least we won't have to worry about the bank robbers hanging around."

Unless they pretend to be reporters, Jaime thought.

Chapter Twenty-Two

Next morning, the satellite van was still parked in their driveway, although most of the cars that had been parked at the curb were gone.

"We need to get into the house," their mother said. "School starts in three days and my vacation ends tomorrow."

"And mine." Dad pulled along the curb. The moment the car doors opened, a group of reporters rushed forward with microphones and cameras.

Jaime steeled herself for more questions.

"Are you the young lady who was lost in the Sierras?"

"It was actually at a lower elevation," her father said, gripping Jaime's shoulders to reassure her.

"I used my Girl Scout survival training and what my father taught me. It's really no big deal." She started for the house.

"Wait a minute." The reporters trailed after her. "Everyone in the country was worried about you. Don't you think you owe them an explanation?"

Jaime turned and planted both hands on her hips. "I was taking pictures of animals when I got lost. I covered myself with branches and leaves to stay warm at night and I ate berries. I started a fire with my camera lens and the rangers rescued me with their helicopter. That's all there is to tell."

"Wow, that's quite a story. Were you afraid?" The microphone was inches from her nose.

"Only when the bears came past and an animal growled near my campsite. But I scared him away with my camera flash."

"Talk shows hosts will be scrambling to interview you."

Sam stepped forward. "I was in the search party."

The reporters ignored him while peppering Jaime with questions, including whether she had been seen by a doctor.

"I saw one at the clinic yesterday. He said I'm in great shape, except for a few scratches from the berry bushes."

"That's enough," her father said. "We're still tired from the ordeal." He nudged Jaime and Sam toward the house.

Once inside and the door locked behind them, they all sat down in the living room.

"You handled that well, dear," Grandma said. "How does it feel to be famous?"

"I don't like it. I wish they would leave me alone."

"They will in time, but I'm afraid that young reporter is right. The talk show hosts will be calling to have you on their programs."

"Cool," Danny said, bouncing on the couch.

"Not. How would you like people with microphones and cameras following you around?"

126

Her youngest brother shrugged his shoulders and sat very still.

"Jaime can't miss school," her mother said.

"But what if Ellen DeGeneres wants to interview her?" Grandma always watched "The Ellen Show."

Her parents glanced at one another and smiled. "Doesn't matter who asks, she can't miss classes."

Jaime couldn't remember seeing her father quite so serious.

"Well, now that's settled, we need to unpack the car." Grandma struggled to her feet and headed for the foyer. "Who's going to help?"

"We'll do it," Danny said, catching up with her.

Sam peeked out the front window. "They're gone."

Jaime laughed when she noticed the disappointment on his face.

"I'm sure they'll be back."

Grandma frowned. "I hope not, dear. I'm not sure I can stand more excitement."

"I nominate Sam as the family spokesman," Jaime said. "All in favor, raise your hands."

Six hands raised and the matter was settled. Samuel J. Hamilton was officially elected and his grin was as wide as a Frisbee.

"No running out the door at the first sign of a broadcast truck," Dad warned. "We still don't know where the bank robbers are."

"Yes, sir," Sam said, reaching for a notepad and pen on the telephone stand. "I need to make some notes so I'm prepared."

The rest of the family looked at one another and shook their heads. Sam was taking his new job much too seriously, which made Jaime regret his nomination. What would he tell the news media that might embarrass the family?

"I'd like to see your notes when you're finished." She wondered whether Sam would say that he fought off a bear to rescue her. He had a great imagination and would probably write a book someday.

The phone rang, interrupting her thoughts. Jaime answered and was surprised to hear Officer O'Connell's deep voice. "That you, Jaime? The most famous girl in the nation right now?"

She cringed, wishing everyone would forget about her. "Yes, sir. It's me and I'm fine."

"Glad to hear it. I need to speak to your parents, Jaime."

Jaime handed the phone to her father. A lump rose in her throat and she hurried to her bedroom before her first tear fell. Miranda was at her heels and nearly had her tail caught in the closing door. Sitting on the floor, Jaime hugged the shepherd and cried into her thick furry coat.

"What am I going to do, Miranda? Everyone at school will be asking questions. I'll feel like a freak. Maybe it would be better to be locked up in jail so the bank robbers can't find us."

Miranda chuffed softly as though consoling her.

"But what will happen to you while we're gone?"

The dog backed away and stood staring at her.

"You're not thinking of running away are you, girl?"

Miranda shook her head and sneezed.

"Maybe that's not a bad idea. If we run away, the TV reporters can't find us and neither will the bank robbers."

Chapter Twenty-Three

Someone knocked at Jaime's door but she didn't want to answer.

"Jaime?" her mother said from the other side. "May I come in?"

She hesitated before giving her consent.

When the door opened, her mother's expression was sympathetic. "We're not going into protective custody," she said. "You needn't worry about that."

"But Officer O'Connell said–"

"Your father explained what a hardship it would cause and that we might lose our jobs. And you children have to go to school."

"Don't forget Miranda and Grandma." Jaime couldn't imagine Grandma in protective custody, whatever that meant. A jail cell? Or a room with no windows they might all have to share, with guards at the door.

"But who's going to protect us, Mom?"

"We'll have a police guard. In fact, three rotating guards twenty-four-hours a day."

"In uniform with guns?"

"I imagine so."

"That's cool."

"Your brothers think so."

"Samuel J. Hamilton will probably talk them crazy."

"Don't be so hard on your brother. He doesn't realize how annoying showing off his intelligence can be."

"If he's so smart, why can't he figure out a way to trap the bank robbers?"

Her mother sighed. "He says he's working on that."

"I hope he's not building traps like the iron on the door."

"Your father talked to him about dangerous traps."

"Good, I don't want to worry about minefields in my own house."

"Why don't you check to make sure all the windows are securely locked while I help your grandmother unpack."

Jaime had some unpacking of her own to do. Later, while checking the window locks, she would think about ways to protect her family. Sam wasn't the only smart member of the Hamilton clan. Miranda trailed along behind her as she checked each window. Reaching down to pet her, Jaime smiled to herself, remembering that Miranda had avoided her when she first arrived. The boys considered her *their* dog, but the shepherd stayed at *her* side, not theirs.

Sam was sitting at the dining room table drawing.

"Figured out a plan, yet, Mister Genius?"

"I'm working on it," he said, without looking up.

"Don't antagonize your brother," Grandma said. "He's trying his best to help us."

Jaime stared at the carpet. *Grandma must think I'm terrible*. Arguing with Sam was a habit she needed to break. "Sorry," she mumbled and went back to checking windows.

At the front window she glanced out at the street, glad there were no more strange cars parked at the curb or broadcast vans in the driveway. A moment later she noticed a dusty black car slowly drive by. Their window was so dirty that she couldn't see the driver, but he was obviously looking at her through a clean peephole in the glass. Ducking below the window sill, she crawled into the dining room.

"Mom, Dad," she croaked, "those men just drove by. I was afraid they were going to stop and shoot me through the window."

Her father dropped a suitcase and hurried into the living room. "Where are they? I don't see anyone?" He then opened the entry door.

"Be careful, Harold," Grandma warned. "We'd better call the police."

Sam followed his father onto the narrow porch. "Jaime probably imagined them. You know what a fraidy cat she is."

"That's enough," his father scolded. "Jaime proved how brave she is while lost in the mountains. I don't want to hear either one of you talking badly about the other. Do you hear?"

Sam hung his head.

Dad and Grandma were right, Jaime thought. No more arguing, no matter what Sam said to her. They had more important things to do.

Where was Danny? She hurried down the hall to look in the boys' room. He wasn't there. Maybe the kitchen. Danny was nowhere to be found. When she told her parents, they scattered, calling her brother's name. As soon as they knew he wasn't in the house, Dad went outside, cautioning them to stay behind.

A moment later he returned with Danny in tow. Her brother held tightly to a huge glass jar which contained the largest spider she had ever seen. A tarantula!

Grinning, he said, "I told you I could trap one."

"How'd you do it?" Sam seemed as excited as Danny.

"Piece a cake."

"What?"

"I used a piece of Mom's chocolate cake."

"Tarantula's like chocolate?"

Danny smirked at his brother. "If you're so smart, you should have known that."

Dad took the jar and placed it on the kitchen counter. "Don't ever give chocolate to Miranda. Chocolate can be deadly to dogs."

"I won't, Dad. I promise." Danny got to his knees and hugged the shepherd.

"Can we keep the tarantula?" Sam asked.

"Spiders don't make good pets. And how would you like to live in a small enclosed space?"

"We can put him in a fish tank."

"We'll see."

Danny was standing at the kitchen counter, gazing fondly at the tarantula. "He can scare the bank robbers away."

"How?"

"Frisky can jump on them."

"Frisky? Is that what you named him?" Sam was clearly amused.

"How do you know it's a male spider, son?"

"Easy. He lifted his leg inside the jar."

Chapter Twenty-Four

The first officer arrived half an hour later. Tall, young and lean, he resembled one of Jaime's teachers. She looked twice to make sure that her math teacher had not joined the police force. She would ask him later if he had a brother who taught at Cherrywood Middle School.

When he stepped into the house to introduce himself, Danny asked if he could hold his gun.

"Never touch a dangerous weapon because it could hurt someone," Officer Drake explained. "Children as well as adults have been killed with guns they thought weren't loaded."

Danny thought about that for a moment. He then said, "Want to see my tarantula?"

"Uh, sure. Where are you keeping it?"

"In the kitchen, of course." Taking the officer's hand, he led him to the counter.

"Nice spider, Danny, but don't you think you should turn it loose. Unless the tarantula has committed a crime, you shouldn't keep him in jail."

"He stole a piece of chocolate cake."

The policeman laughed. "That's a misdemeanor, not a felony. He shouldn't be locked up for that."

"But he's going to help us catch the bank robbers."

"Promise me you'll turn him loose as soon as we arrest the suspects."

Danny chewed his lip and looked again at Frisky. "Okay, I'll let him go as soon as you catch the bad guys."

The officer tousled Danny's hair and followed him into the dining room. Jaime and Sam were sitting at the table using the Ouija board.

"What's that you're playing?"

"We're not playing, sir," Sam said, without looking up. "This is serious business. The Ouija channels messages from outer space."

"Ah, I see. Messages from Mars?"

Jaime laughed. "Bagnomi didn't tell us where he's from. Maybe we should ask him."

The planchette circled the board several times before it spelled out T-H-E O-T-H-E-R W-O-R-L-D.

"The Other World? I never heard of that one. Ask your friend where it's located."

Bagnomi spelled T-H-R-E-E F-E-E-T A-B-O-V-E Y-O-U.

"Three feet above you? How can that be?"

The planchette was moving again. This time it spelled I-N A-N-O-T-H-E-R D-I-M-E-N-S-I-O-N.

"Oh, well," the officer said. "That explains it. Bagnomi's in another dimension."

"Wherever he is, he's always right."

"No one's *always* right."

"Bagnomi is. Ask him a question."

Officer Drake thought for a moment before he asked, "How many toes do I have?"

Bagnomi spelled "F-O-U-R A-N-D A H-A-L-F O-N L-E-F-T A-N-D H–O-L-E I-N S-O-C-K.

"Four and half on left and hole in sock," Sam said laughing.

The officer coughed and his face turned red.

"He's right, isn't he?" Sam was smirking.

"It's time to have a look around outside. I'll see you kids later."

Jaime frowned a warning for Sam not to laugh. But as soon as the front door closed, they both covered their mouths and giggled.

Placing their fingers back on the plachette, Jaime asked, "Where are the bank robbers?"

N-O-T F-A-R A-W-A-Y.

"In our neighborhood?"

Yes.

"Will they try again to kidnap us?"

Yes.

"When?"

T-O-N-I-G-H-T.

"Oh my gosh, I knew it."

Jaime sighed. "We have police protection but we can't tell them Bagnomi told us."

"Officer Drake will believe Bagnomi. That is, *if* he has a hole in his sock."

139

"You're right. We'd better tell him."

"He'll probably go off duty before tonight. What if the policeman who replaces him doesn't believe us?"

"We'll have him ask a question."

"What if Bagnomi goes off duty by then?"

"We'll ask his replacement."

Sam rose from his chair. "We'd better tell Office Drake before it's too late."

Jaime followed him to the front door. They had been warned not to leave the house without an adult, but this was important. The policeman was not in the yard. She scanned the street in both directions, fearful the dusty black car was parked nearby.

"He must be out back." Sam jumped from the steps and ran toward the side yard, leaving Jaime alone on the narrow front porch.

"Sam!" Undecided whether to follow, Jaime hesitated before she took off after him. She found him babbling to the officer near the garage.

"And they're coming to get us tonight."

Officer Drake planted his large hand on Sam's shoulder. "Hold on, son. You can't believe everything the Ouija board tells you."

"If you have a hole in your sock, we do."

The officer looked skyward, sighing heavily.

"Well?"

"Okay, I was in a hurry this morning and–oh, never mind, let's go back in the house."

Sam glanced at Jaime with an "I-told -you-so" expression.

Once the door closed behind them, the officer asked to speak to their parents.

"They're unpacking in the bedroom." Sam hurried down the hall.

"Don't worry about all this, young lady. That's what the police department is for, to protect you and your family."

"I wish I knew why those men are so anxious to kidnap us. If I were them, I would get as far away from here as possible. Wouldn't you?"

Before he could answer, Jaime's father came down the hall, followed by her mother.

"What's this Sam's telling us? The bank robbers are still hanging around?"

"A possibility, Mr. Hamilton."

"But they must be crazy to stay in the area."

Crazy enough to try to break into the house, Jaime thought as she made her way to the front window.

Chapter Twenty-Five

"Nobody out there that I can see." Jaime closed the drapes and turned to face the others.

"They'll probably wait till dark," Sam said.

"After bedtime." Danny was holding Frisky's jar.

"Be careful not to drop that, son."

"I won't, Dad. Not till the bad guys come."

Everyone exchanged worried glances.

"Make sure it isn't one of us coming into your bedroom, Danny."

"How about a password? 'Don't let Frisky go.'"

"Good idea."

Jaime leaned closer to examine the tarantula. "What do you plan to feed Frisky, besides chocolate cake?"

"No more cake," Mom said. "It might make him sick."

"I'll look it up on the Internet." Sam stood to leave the room.

Excusing herself, Jaime followed him down the hall.

Once in his room, Sam booted up the computer and typed TARANTULA into the search box. He then scrolled down the page until he found the site he was looking for. The Wikipedia page said: *The largest tarantulas may kill small vertebrates, but their usual food is other arthropods.*

Jaime leaned over his shoulder. "What are vertebrates? Other arthropods must mean they eat spiders."

"Didn't you learn about vertebrates in biology class?"

"Probably, but I forgot."

"At least you were right about anthropoids. They're arachnids. spiders, mites, crustaceans, millipedes, centipedes, insects–"

"Okay, Mister. Encyclopedia, where are we going to find arachnids and vertebrates, if we can't leave the house?"

Sam thought for a moment before answering. "Put out some of mom's chocolate cake on the back steps and hope some insects come along."

"Miranda might take a bite and get sick."

"You're right. We'll put something else out to attract the bugs."

"Flies attract spiders. But how do we catch flies?"

"Fly paper. We can buy some at the hardware store."

"That's a lot of trouble for a silly old tarantula."

"Frisky's not silly and he might scare off the robbers."

"Do you really believe that, Sam?"

"What would you do if a tarantula jumped on you?"

"Scream and probably faint."

"Let's hope the robbers will, if they break in tonight."

144

"What else does it say about tarantulas?"

"It says their bite may be painful but it's not usually dangerous to humans."

"I'm glad to hear that."

"Some Asian spiders are called tarantulas but they're more like a scorpion without a tail. They used to be called wolf spiders and they lived in southern Europe. The tarantula's bite was supposed to cause tarantism, a nervous condition that caused hysteria."

"Yikes. I hope Frisky isn't Asian. I'm nervous enough already."

"It says the best cure was believed to be strenuous and prolonged dancing of the tarantella."

"What does that mean?"

Sam typed in TARANTELLA, which brought up a description of an Italian dance. He read: The tarantella was danced alone by a victim of a tarantula bite, and lasted for hours or even days.

"Dancing can cure a tarantula bite?"

"That's what it says. If Frisky bites us, we'll have to take dancing lessons."

"He's not getting close enough to bite me."

"We'll see." Sam turned his head to smirk at her.

"You wouldn't?"

"I might."

"I'll tell Dad."

"It won't be my fault if Danny drops the jar."

"You'd trip him so he'd fall and break the jar?"

Someone knocked at the door. Dad's voice said, "Come out here, you two. Hurry."

Their father beckoned them into the living room where the television set was on. Photos of two rough-looking men were on the screen.

"That's them," Danny yelled.

Jaime only had a brief look before the screen changed and a police officer began talking about the bank robbers

"We were right," Sam said.

"Apparently so. At least now everyone knows what they look like." Dad switched off the TV set and told his children to be seated. Clearing his throat, he said, "I talked to Officer Drake again. He thinks that we should go into protective custody for a few days until they catch the criminals."

"But, what if they don't catch them before school starts?" Jaime felt a lump in her throat.

"An officer will escort you to school and back again."

"Back to where, Dad?"

"Wherever we're going to stay."

"But what about Grandma and Miranda?"

"They'll come too."

"What if the robbers break into the house?"

"Our alarm system will connect with the police department."

"When?"

"Tomorrow morning. It's all arranged."

Danny clutched the jar to his chest. "Can Frisky come too?"

146

"I don't think so, son. You'll have to let the tarantula go."

Danny's lips trembled and he hurried toward his room. A moment later they heard a loud crash and the house trembled.

Chapter Twenty-Six

Grandma clutched her blouse, saying, "Oh, my heavens, what was that?"

Dad had already started down the hall when Danny opened his door, screaming. When he was finally able to speak, he said, "Something crashed into my bedroom wall and scared me."

Once inside the room, Dad looked around but could find no damage.

"Be careful," Danny warned. "I dropped the jar and Frisky jumped out. He's probably under the bed."

Dad closed the door and warned everyone to stay out of the boys' room. "Stay put while I go out to investigate." He then picked up the baseball bat by the door and took it with him.

Maybe protective custody wasn't such a bad idea. Especially if it didn't include Frisky. How would they lure him out of the bedroom without being attacked? Jaime imagined herself dancing the tarantella for days before dropping exhausted to the floor.

"We'd better start packing," her mother said.

Sam stamped his foot. "We just unpacked and we can't get in our room. Frisky might bite us."

"We'll trick him out of our room with chocolate cake." Danny said.

"Don't let Miranda near the cake," Grandma warned, clutching the dog's collar.

"There's a cardboard box in the garage. We can cut a hole and put the cake inside."

"Yeah, Sam. As soon as Frisky goes in, we'll cover the hole with tape."

"It's almost dark. I think you should wait for your father to get the box."

"It will only take a second," Sam told his mother. The boys raced out the kitchen door before she could say another word.

When they returned, Mom said, "The longer we wait the hungrier Frisky will be. Don't spiders feed at night?"

"I'll check." Sam started down the hall.

Danny laughed. "Frisky's probably using the computer."

Grandma shook her bright red curls and frowned. "Isn't anyone curious about that loud noise we heard?"

"Maybe it was Frisky's jar hitting the floor."

"Don't be silly, Danny. That wouldn't shake the entire house."

"What do you think happened?"

"Maybe the bank robbers' car hit the house, or maybe they threw explosives in the yard. Maybe it was a sonic boom."

"I'll wait till Dad gets back to find out what happened."

Mom told them to gather at the kitchen table. She would make them a batch of chocolate chip cookies.

"Before dinner?" Danny's grin was wide.

"We're not going to make a habit of it. Just this once."

Maybe Frisky would like one too. Jaime imagined the huge spider eating a cookie his own size.

The entry door opened and Dad and the policemen stepped inside. Sirens screamed in the distance. "Nothing for us to worry about," her father said. "There was some sort of explosion down near the highway.

"Was anyone hurt, Dad?"

"We don't know yet."

While Dad was telling Mom and Grandma about the explosion, Jaime followed her brothers down the hall. Sam used his pocketknife to cut a small hole in the side of the box and Danny crumbled the cookie and placed a bit of cake inside. They then carefully opened the bedroom door. Frisky was nowhere in sight, so the box was shoved inside and the door quickly closed.

"How long are we going to wait?" Jaime whispered.

Checking his watch, Sam said, "Half an hour should do it. I'm not sure if tarantulas can smell food but he must be hungry by now."

"You can use my laptop to research if spiders can smell." Jaime started for her own bedroom.

"Good idea." Sam grinned as he started to follow.

"When do I get a laptop?" Danny whined.

"When you get all A's on your report card, like Jaime and I did."

"Grandma will buy me one too?"

151

"Why don't you ask her?"

Danny scampered down the hall to talk to his grandmother.

They both sat on Jaime's bed and Sam booted up her computer. "Do you think your plan's going to work, Sam?"

"It's worth a try. We can't let Frisky roam around the house."

Jaime wouldn't be able to sleep. Thoughts of those bent hairy legs crawling over her body would send her into hysterics. And if Frisky bit her, would the tarantella dance really work? She didn't think so. It was a silly superstition. But, if it didn't work, why write about it on the Internet? Cold chills raced up her arms.

Jaime was glad that Frisky was too big to crawl beneath the door. There was no place to hide from a tarantula. They could jump as high as six feet and land on Dad's head.

"Find anything?" She peered over Sam's shoulder.

"Yeah, look at this: Most spiders have eight eyes but they don't see very well unless they're jumping spiders, like Frisky. They get their feelings from the hairs on their legs. Different kinds of hairs help them touch and taste things and even hear. And their noses are on their feet.

"They walk on their noses?"

"They have small pits on their feet that can pick up scents of things to eat. And they can even smell their enemies."

"Great, then Frisky can smell the chocolate."

"Let's hope he doesn't remember that chocolate landed him in Danny's glass jail."

Jaime laughed. "I wonder how far away from the chocolate he can smell."

"If his nose is on his foot, he may have to walk on top of it before he gets the scent."

"Maybe we should sprinkle some chocolate chips leading to the box."

"Are you volunteering?"

Jaime shook her head. It was a good idea but she wasn't willing to risk a tarantula bite. Someone braver would have to do it.

Chapter Twenty-Seven

"If we make a trail of chocolate chips," Sam said, "Frisky won't be hungry enough to go inside the box."

Jaime groaned. "I didn't think of that."

"I wonder where Danny and I'll sleep tonight if Frisky doesn't cooperate."

"Sleeping bags, I guess."

Jaime remembered hearing of children taken from their beds in the middle of the night.

"Sleeping bags are a good idea. If we're all together in the living room, they can't kidnap us while we're sleeping in our beds." She reminded him what Bagnomi had said about a possible break-in that night.

"Grandma can sleep on the couch," Sam said, "And Miranda can stand guard."

When they told Dad their plan, he thought for a moment. "Actually, that's not a bad idea, whether Bagnomi is right or not. And it would only last for one night."

"What about the tarantula, Harold?" Grandma's face looked worried.

"We'll find a way to trap him in the morning when there's more light."

Sam placed a finger to his lips when Danny started to tell about the box. Jaime knew Sam wanted to prove to his father how brave he was by trapping Frisky on his own. Grabbing a flashlight, Sam accompanied Dad to the garage to retrieve the sleeping bags while Jaime stayed to help her mother prepare dinner. It was twilight when she scraped the plates and placed them in the dishwasher.

When the grownups settled in the living room to watch television, Sam whispered, "Time to see if Frisky took the bait."

They followed him down the hall. Jaime's heart thumped when Sam opened the door and switched on the light. He shook his head to let the others know that Frisky was nowhere in sight. He then stooped to grasp the box. Turning it so that the hole was facing the ceiling, he quickly backed from the room and closed the door.

"He's in the box. Quick, Danny with the tape."

Danny placed a length of wide gray tape over the hole and pressed it tightly into the cardboard to prevent Frisky from jumping out.

"What are we going to do with him?" Jaime asked.

"We'll put the box on the back porch and pull the tape off the hole so Frisky can jump out and go home as soon as we close the door."

"But what if Frisky gets hurt?" Danny wasn't so sure about the plan.

"Frisky can take care of himself."

"But he depends on us for chocolate cake and cookies."

"Chocolate wasn't made for spiders or animals, Danny. And Frisky will be much happier with other tarantulas. He might even have a family."

"You mean little tarantulas at home?"

"Yes. Now let's put Frisky outside so he can go home."

"Okay, Jaime. He can tell his kids how brave he was."

Sam set the box on the porch, pulled the tape and locked the back door.

"Bedtime," Mom called.

Their parents had pushed the furniture aside to make room for the sleeping bags. Everyone then spread their bags on the living room floor and crawled into them in their clothes, in case of an emergency. Jaime soon heard her father softly snoring and knew that her brothers were also asleep. She heard Grandma groan as she turned over on the couch. She gasped when something wet and cold touched her cheek.

"Lie down, Miranda," she whispered, hoping not to wake the others.

She lay awake wondering where the policeman was stationed. Was he in his patrol car or out walking around to insure that no one tried to break in? She couldn't crawl from her sleeping bag to peer out the windows because she might step on a family member in the dark.

Miranda chuffed softly and lay across Jaime's ankles. Knowing the dog was there made her feel safe and she finally fell asleep. But her sleep was troubled with dreams of being chased across the apron of Spider Mountain. She stumbled and fell into a thick bed of lupines before she began to roll toward the street. Someone reached out to grab her before she hit the pavement and she screamed when a deep voice said, "Where do you think you're going, little lady?"

Jaime awoke and sat up in her sleeping bag. Had she screamed aloud? She sat listening to the sounds of her sleeping family. Thank goodness she hadn't awakened them. But what was that noise? She closed her eyes and strained to determine if it was coming from the porch off the kitchen. She was disoriented in the dark and couldn't remember which direction her sleeping bag was facing.

She heard a thump and a man's voice yelling. Where was the policeman?

"Dad," she said, "Wake up. Something's happening outside."

"Huh?" she heard in the dark.

"Dad, please wake up. Frisky must have bitten one of the bank robbers."

The boys were awake and trying to remove themselves from their sleeping bags. "Are you sure, Jaime?" Danny said.

"Sorry to wake you, but I know what I heard."

"Stay put, everyone, while I take a look outside."

"Be careful, dear." Mom sounded worried.

The doorbell rang. Dad switched on the porch light and opened the front door.

A man's voice said, "Mr. Hamilton, we have the men in custody. That was a smart move putting the tarantula in the box."

The boys yelled in triumph as Jaime blinked back at the light shining in her eyes.

Danny was jumping on his sleeping bag. "Frisky caught the bank robbers."

Dad looked around in confusion. "I don't understand."

"One of the suspects tripped over the box when he was trying to unlock your kitchen door. He yelled and we caught both him and his partner."

Sam puffed up his narrow chest. "Danny and I caught Frisky and put in him in the box."

"When?"

Both boys talked at once.

Shaking his head, their father said, "I'm proud of you both but you should have asked for my help."

"I helped too," Jaime said, feeling left out.

"I'm proud of all of you," he said, gathering them into a group hug. "But next time . . ."

"We know." Jaime hugged him. "We'll ask for your help."

Out of the corner of her eye, Jaime saw something small and dark creep into the foyer while Dad was talking to the policeman. No, it can't be.

Chapter Twenty-Eight

"Frisky!" Danny yelled.

"Stay back, son." Dad reached down to grasp the tarantula as it crawled past. Taking a couple of steps to the porch, he stooped to set the spider down. A second later he yelped in pain.

"Frisky bit Dad," Sam said. "Now he'll have to dance the tarantella."

Mom nearly tripped over her sleeping bag in her hurry to reach her husband. "Is it a bad bite, dear?"

Their father stood shaking his hand as though something sticky were clinging to it. "Looks like another trip to the emergency room," he said.

"You can tape a penny to the bite like they do for bee stings," Grandma said.

"It might work for bees but I don't think it will cure a spider bite." Dad continued to jerk his hand.

"I'll put on some music."

"I don't think so, son–"

"But, the Wikipedia says the tarantella cures tarantula bites. That's why they call it the tarantella."

Dad reached into his pocket with his uninjured hand for his keys. "Everyone into the car. I'm not taking any chances on ancient cures. I need this hand when I start back to work."

Sam grumbled to himself as he followed the others outside. "I wanted to see if it really worked."

"Samuel J. Hamilton will have to find out another way," Jaime said. "Why don't you find Frisky and let him bite *you*. Then you can dance for days without stopping. I'll even play all your favorite CDs."

When Sam glared at her, she said, "I can't wait to tell all your friends at school about your cure for tarantula bites. They'll make you dance the tarantella until you fall on the school ground."

"You wouldn't."

Jaime crossed her arms and lifted her chin to imitate her brother. "Am I the smartest and bravest sister you ever knew?"

"Okay, Jaime." He hung his head. "You win."

"And are you proud of me?"

"I guess so."

"You won't argue and challenge my authority anymore?"

"That's asking a lot, don't you think?"

"Okay, we'll compromise," Jaime said.

"How's that?"

"Today we won't argue or fight."

"And tomorrow?"

"Tomorrow we'll see how it goes. If we don't argue all day I'll give you my favorite CD."

"And if we argue?"

"You'll give me your favorite?"

"Sounds like a plan," Danny said from nearby.

"Yes, it does." Dad motioned them into the car.

"What about Frisky?" Danny wailed.

"I'm sure he's well on his way back up the hill to his home."

"It's not a hill, Dad," Jaime said. "It's Spider Mountain. Thank goodness we solved the mystery of who lives at the summit."

"No more Spider Mountain adventures," Mom warned, as the car pulled away from the curb.

"We learned our lesson," Jaime said. *But our next adventure will be our trip to Crimson Dawn when we visit Uncle Harry next summer. Then we'll know if there's really a ghost who lives there.*

Read an excerpt from the next Hamilton Kids' mystery novel, *The Ghost of Crimson Dawn.*

The Ghost of Crimson Dawn

The drive up the narrow mountain road seemed to last forever and the Hamilton kids were anxious to reach the ranch.

Sam leaned to peer through the windshield. "Wow! What was that?"

"That's a deer that jumped the fence," Uncle Harry slowed the car even more so they could have a better look.

His ranch was nestled in the Laramie Mountains. He and Aunt Silly had no children of their own and they doted on the Hamilton kids whenever they visited them in California. Jaime, Sam, and Danny had flown to Wyoming with their grandmother and were excited to spend a month at the ranch.

They loved Uncle Harry, who was as bald as an eagle's egg and round as an exercise ball. His huge graying mustache always had bits and pieces of his latest meal stuck to its graying ends. And their beloved Aunt Silly—whose real name was Sylvia—was as small as her husband was large. Her brown hair was pulled high on her head into a large bun and her green eyes sparkled whenever she smiled, which was often.

"What would you kids like to see first," their uncle asked when they pulled up to the house. "The ghost of Crimson Dawn," nine-year old Danny said.

His uncle laughed. "You can't see ghosts in the daylight, son. That will have to wait."

Danny hung his head and looked so pathetic that Aunt Silly tousled his hair. "How about one of my home baked cookies?"

That produced a grin.

Sam scooted to the edge of his chair. "When can we go to Crimson Dawn?"

"We can go on Saturday, after the chores are done?"

Sam nodded but his lower lip stuck out.

"How old are you now, Sam?" Aunt Silly asked.

"Eleven going on forty," his grandmother answered for him. "He surprises me with all that he knows."

"Sam's a walking encyclopedia," his sister Jaime said. She was two years older than her brother Sam, although they were almost the same height. "You wouldn't believe what comes out of his mouth."

Uncle Harry laughed again. "You've all grown faster than mustard green stalks."

Grandma shook her bright red curls and said, "I almost didn't recognize them when I moved in last summer. They were in the process of capturing two bank robbers."

"Bank robbers?" Harry and Sylvia's eyebrows shot toward their hairlines.

"On Spider Mountain," Danny said.

"We tracked them with our Ouija Board," Sam puffed up his narrow chest.

"You're joking." This time their uncle didn't laugh.

"We'll tell you about it later," Grandma said. "First, we need to unpack."

Both boys groaned. Jaime knew they were itching to go outside and chase Aunt Silly's geese.

Later that afternoon as they were exploring the hillside ranch, they spotted a tan and white animal in the distance.

"Sit down and don't move," Sam whispered.

Danny wanted to know why.

"It's a pronghorn antelope."

Danny snorted. "It's got horns. Maybe it's a deer."

"Look at its big head. It's not streamlined like a deer."

Danny just stared.

Sam placed his hand on his brother's shoulder and they both sat down in the weeds. "They're curious animals and they'll come right up to you if you don't move and scare them away."

"You sure?"

"I read about it in a wildlife magazine."

Jaime sat on a flat rock nearby and slowly raised a camera to her eyes.

"No flash," Sam warned. "It'll scare the antelope away."

"I learned that while I was lost in the Sierra foothills," Jaime checked her camera and whispered back. "The flash probably saved me from being eaten by a bear."

"Shhhhh," Sam warned. "He's coming this way."

"How can you tell it's a he?" Danny whispered back.

"Look at his antlers."

"Don't girl antelope have antlers?"

3

"Some have small horns."

They watched the antelope take his time moving in their direction, stopping several times to nibble dried grass. As he came nearer, the boys crouched lower in the weeds. Jaime joined them by slowly sliding from the rock, her camera at the ready. What if the animal lowered his head and charged them with his antlers? Jaime wasn't so sure they should be sitting there. She whispered her fears to Sam.

"Antelopes are scaredy cats," Sam said. "If I wave my arms, he'll run way."

Jaime gulped back her fear. Glancing at Danny, she saw that his eyes were huge. So she wasn't the only one afraid of the antelope. If they stayed where they were, would it come right up and sniff them? She didn't want to stay around to find out. When the animal was within ten feet, she raised her camera and clicked off a picture. The sound started the antelope and it wheeled and raced away, its white backside growing smaller in the distance.

"Why'd you do that?" Sam said, angry.

"That's what cameras are for."

Both boys stood and watched the antelope disappear over a rise.

"Sweet," Danny said. "He can run faster than Dad can drive the car."

"They have to run fast," his brother explained. "In Africa, they have to run away from lions and cheetahs."

"Don't forget the bears and bob cats that roam the mountains here that Uncle Harry warned us about," Jaime said.

As they were climbing back up the slope, they saw several animals in the opposite direction. Jaime zoomed her

4

camera lens. When the animals came into focus, she gasped. "They're huge and have antlers like small trees."

Sam took the camera and looked for himself. "We'd better get back to the house."

"Why?" Danny whined.

"Those look like elk. They're a lot bigger than antelope and they've been known to charge people. Especially smaller ones like us."

Scurrying up the rise to the ranch house, they turned to look back. Instead of sliding under a wire fence as the antelope had done or jumping over like deer, the elk charged right through.

Danny frowned."Uncle Harry isn't going to be happy that the elk tore down his fence."

Sam handed the camera back to Jaime. "Looks like they're heading for the watering hole."

Within a short distance of the house, they sat for a while watching three elk drink from the pond. They then charged through another fence and into a pasture where the cattle grazed. The cows didn't even raise their heads to look at the newcomers.

The boys agreed they'd like to live on the ranch.

Jaime gasped. "What about Mom and Dad?"

Danny rubbed the freckles on his nose. "They could come and visit."

"What about Miranda?"

They decided they'd miss their Australian Shepherd if they stayed away too long. They also admitted they'd miss their parents.

"That's better." Jaime checked her watch. "It's almost dinner time. We'd better go inside."

5

Uncle Harry sat on the front porch watching the sun's afterglow. When they told him the elk had taken down his fence, he said the boys could help him string new wire the following day. He didn't appear to be upset.

Jaime was surprised. "Barbed wire?"

"Oh, no, we don't want to harm the animals."

"But wouldn't it keep the elk from tearing down your fences?"

"No, it would only cause them pain."

They found Grandma in the kitchen with Aunt Silly. Both women were laughing and Grandma's bright red curls trembled.

"She looks like a little Ronald McDonald," Danny whispered

Jaime smiled. They were lucky to have such a fun grandmother who liked to play games. Aunt Silly was fun too but she wasn't very good at playing games.

Saturday was three days away and they would have to wait to find out about the ghost of Crimson Dawn.

Chapter 2

Next morning the boys were up before the sun. A tantalizing aroma snaked in from the kitchen and infiltrated their room. Aunt Silly and Grandma must be cooking something special.

"I smell bacon frying," Danny hopped out of his narrow bunk and opened the bedroom door.

Sam's stomach growled in anticipation. "Pancakes too, I'll betcha."

Danny was already dressed and out of their room before Sam could pull on his jeans. He then noticed that his younger brother had forgotten to wear his shoes. Sam picked them up and tossed them under the beds. Danny could find them later.

Uncle Harry's huge mustache lifted above a wide grin when Sam entered the room. "Flapjacks are ready. Grab a plate and fill it up." Motioning Sam to join him and Danny at the large round kitchen table, he pushed a jar of molasses in his direction.

Sam stared at the thick dark syrup and shook his head. "I like honey better, sir."

"No problem. We've got jams and jellies and all kinds of good stuff that kids like." He pushed back his chair and rummaged through a cupboard.

Aunt Silly turned from the stove with a plate full of steaming pancakes. "There's more where these came from." Dividing them between Sam and Danny, she watched them pour honey and syrup on their hotcakes.

Uncle Harry ate his last bite and scooped more pancakes onto his plate. "By the way, kids, where did you hear about the ghost of Crimson Dawn?"

"On the Internet," Sam said between mouths full. "There was a story about Casper Mountain but not much about the ghost."

"Really? Well, isn't that something?" Uncle Harry laid his fork aside. "I've lived here most of my life and I never heard about the ghost until a few years ago."

Grandma came to the table holding a plate of sausage. "That's all I've heard about for weeks. You would think that ghost was a rock star."

Danny laughed. "A rock star ghost is funny, Grandma."

Jaime appeared at the kitchen door, yawning, her long blond hair tangled about her shoulders. Her blue eyes were sleepy and she looked as though she had dressed in a hurry.

"You must be hungry." Aunt Silly pulled a chair away from the table and invited her to sit.

Grandma then filled her plate with sausage, eggs and pancakes.

"I heard Danny laughing. What's so funny this early in the morning?" Jaime yawned again.

"A rock star ghost," Danny said.

"Are you talking about Jim Morrison?"

8

Aunt Silly smiled. "I remember him. He passed away when I was in high school."

Uncle Harry nodded. "And I remember some of his songs. 'Dawn's Highway' and 'Ghost Song.'"

Sam's fork clattered on his plate. "I never thought of that. You don't suppose—?"

"That he's the ghost of Crimson Dawn?" Jaime finished for him. "What would his ghost be doing in Wyoming?"

"Writing more songs?"

"For who, the other ghosts?"

Danny laughed so hard that he spit his eggs back onto his plate. Grandma rushed to clean up the mess.

Uncle Harry cleared his throat. "Seems to me that Morrison's father was in the navy and they lived on both sea coasts. I doubt the rock star was ever here in the mountains."

Jaime poured syrup on her pancakes. "Then who could the ghost have been in real life, Uncle Harry?"

The older man's eyes twinkled. "It could have been a woman who was hanged with her husband over in Sweetwater County. A rancher wanted their land so some cattleman hanged them from a scrub pine tree."

Jaime gasped. "That's awful."

"Indeed it was. They were innocent people but the rancher swore they were stealing cattle."

"Did they catch the men who hanged them?" Danny wanted to know.

"They did but a judge turned 'em loose."

Jaime looked puzzled. "So you think that the woman who was hanged came here as a ghost to live in the mountains?"

"I wouldn't be surprised."

Sam said, "I thought it was a man ghost."

"Maybe it was her husband," Danny said.

Uncle Harry smiled as though he had a secret. "Could be."

Danny leaned across his plate. "Or maybe they take turns ghosting."

All the talk about people dying killed Jaime's appetite. She took her plate to the sink and rinsed it. "Who else could be the ghost, Uncle Harry?"

He scooped the last of his pancakes under his huge mustache. "It could be Charley Eads. He was one of the first people to arrive in this area in a covered wagon with his son and daughter when the railroad line, came to town."

Danny's eyes grew large. "That was a long time ago, wasn't it?"

"Yep, that was back in June of eighteen-eighty-eight."

"But why would he become a ghost?" Jaime asked.

"When gold was discovered, he built a mining camp on top of Casper Mountain. They called it Eadsville."

"That should have made him rich," Sam said.

"But it didn't, you see. When they had the gold tested, they found that it wasn't worth mining."

Jaime sighed. "So the poor man must have been sad."

"I would imagine so."

Grandma and Aunt Silly each took a seat at the table. "What about Caspar Collins?" Aunt Silly said. "The young lieutenant who was killed by the Indians when they attacked the fort. The ghost might be him."

Uncle Harry nodded. "That makes sense."

Grandma looked puzzled. "I thought Crimson Dawn was something in comic books."

"It is, but that has nothing to do with the one on Casper mountain."

Sam looked pleased with himself. "What about the outlaws that used to ride around Wyoming robbing banks and trains. Couldn't it have been one of them?"

"It could but it's not."

Danny rose from his chair to take his uncle's arm. "Then who *is* the ghost, Uncle Harry?"

"Well, there was this woman who told spooky stories about witches and warlocks to her children some seventy or eighty years ago. They lived on the Crimson Dawn Ranch and when she passed away she decided to hang around to haunt the place."

Danny's face fell. "So what's the big deal with that?"

"The big deal is the summer solstice celebration that's held every year at the Crimson Dawn Ranch. Hundreds of people drive up the mountain to see people dressed up like witches and warlocks. And the area around the ranch is still supposed to be haunted by the woman who used to own the place."

Sam hung his head.

"Sorry to disappoint you, Sammy, but that's the rest of the story."

Jaime laughed. Her brother hated to be called Sammy.

"I thought the ghost was someone special."

11

Uncle Harry pushed his plate aside. "From what I hear, the woman was very special. Do you still want to go to the ranch?"

"I guess so."

"I wanna go." Danny jumped up from his chair, almost knocking his plate from the table.

"Me, too," Jaime said. "I can tell my friends about it when we get home."

Danny danced a jig chanting, "Witches and warlocks. Warlocks and witches."

He stopped dancing to stare at Uncle Harry. "What are warlocks?"

"Men witches," Sam said before their uncle could answer.

"That's true, son, but there's more to the story than that. Why don't you look up warlocks on Aunt Silly's computer?"

The Ghost of Crimson Dawn will be available in November 2011.

ABOUT THE AUTHOR

   Jean Henry Mead is the author of 14 books, both fiction
and nonfiction. The mother of five children and
grandmother of seven is a mystery writer. She also writes
historical fiction and is an award-winning photojournalist.
Her web page is located at: www.jeanhenrymead.com.

Made in the USA
Columbia, SC
03 November 2020

23885136R00102